A CRYSTAL DAGGER

KIT EARNSHAW

Edited by Emily Berge

Cover design by Roman Belopolsky

ISBN: 978-1-7369771-2-5

First Edition

CHAPTER ONE

I walked into the restaurant and saw Jackson already seated at a table, beaming up at me. He rose to his feet and wrapped me in a tight hug. I could smell a hint of lime on his neck. It was his way of wearing cologne— a dab of lime essential oil so that it didn't overpower his discerning wolf nose. And it mixed with his natural musk in a way that made my head spin and my fingertips tingle to touch him. It brought me back to taking tequila shots, the lime sharp on my tongue as Jack whisked me back onto the dance floor.

He skated his hands down to my waist, taking me in. "Wow," he said, his grey eyes dancing over me. "You are a stunner, Vi. Like how did I get so lucky?"

"You're not so bad yourself, mister." That was an understatement. I had never been so attracted to someone. There was a charge that felt unbridled between us—pure electricity. And it wasn't just physical. Jackson and I had a mind-body-soul connection.

I knew the old Violet would have rolled her eyes or mimed barfing at that. Turns out, people *can* change. The power of love is real, *yada yada yada*.

I sat down across from my man, just a witch and her werewolf boyfriend out for a celebratory dinner. Totally normal stuff. A waiter came by and dropped off two margaritas on the rocks, mixing perfectly with the scent of lime still clinging to Jackson's neck.

"Hope you don't mind. I went ahead and ordered drinks for us," Jackson said.

"Not at all."

His face spread in the sweetest unstoppable grin as he raised his glass. I followed suit and we clinked them together. "Happy 1 month. I know it's kind of cheesy, but I love you so much and can't imagine anyone else being my mate." My insides still somersaulted whenever he mentioned *mate*.

"*Jack*," I practically cooed. (Again, this is who I was now?) We'd certainly moved fast, but it felt so right. A few weeks of dating led to being mated and here we were, already one month in. Fast and furious, but that's how lycanthropes did things. "That's so sweet. I love you so much. Cheers."

"Cheers to us," he said, and we both took a sip of our margaritas, eyes still on each other.

"*Seven years of bad sex*," we said in unison.

"That won't ever be us," Jackson said, an eyebrow arched playfully.

"Never, ever, ever."

When the waiter swung back by our table, Jack ordered us nachos and soon enough, they were delivered. A platter of crispy tortilla chips piled high with queso, black beans, sour cream, pickled jalapenos, pico de gallo, and shredded lettuce. My stomach growled the minute they hit the table, and I realized I hadn't eaten in hours. I was ravenous.

"Meatless, for my sweet sylph," he said.

"Ah, look at my big wolf man making sacrifices— meat sacrifices of all things!"

"What baby wants baby gets," he teased. I stuck my tongue out, feeling cheeky, before diving into the pile of nachos. I moaned in pleasure as I bit down on a hot chip slathered in cheese and sour cream. Jackson laughed as he watched me. "That good, huh?" I nodded, and he grabbed a chip. He closed his eyes contentedly.

"See?"

"You're right, as per usual."

"Mhmm . . . and that's why they are my favorite nachos in all of Brooklyn."

"I can see why," he said in between bites. He paused and then met my gaze thoughtfully. "Have these been magicked?"

"Maybe . . ." I giggled.

"Oh my god, no wonder. Is this an underground spot that I somehow don't know of?"

"Kind of, but not really. Flora's a witch but a freakin' amazing chef, magic or not. Plenty of witches love this spot, but so does the rest of regular old Brooklyn."

"What's her secret?"

"It's a *secret* for a reason, babe. But I suspect

something to do with the way she makes the queso. Probably a little herbal magic, maybe a special flavor enhancement charm. Could have been cooked in a cauldron with carnelian or some other crystals . . ." I shrugged my shoulders as he listened in fascination.

"Wow," he said as he scooped up another messy chip. "It's kind of crazy how little our communities really know about each other."

"I know . . . I mean, I learned about lycanthropes at the academy and read some books growing up, but it wasn't really about culture or traditions. We're kept kind of separate, I guess."

"Yeah, same. I definitely never thought I'd mate with a witch."

"Oh really?"

"Yeah, I mean, I've gone on dates with witches in the past, but I just never thought I could connect with one the way I connect with you. Kinda just assumed I'd get with another wolf."

"And I just thought I'd live out my Carrie Bradshaw fantasy of being a single girl in the city. Having tons of sex and short episode-long relationships with a bevy of handsome men. But here I am."

"I know, I just had to ruin it for you."

"Seriously." I said, taking a long dramatic sip of my margarita. "It's despicable."

WE ATE our nachos and emptied our margarita glasses before ordering another round. Mushroom quesadilla appeared for me and carnitas enchiladas for Jackson. We played footsie under the table as we ate and drank, talking about our weeks and fantasizing about future plans. In the heat of love and food, my stomach felt as happy as my heart.

I was desperate for a beach vacation and had been drooling over pictures and travel blogs from Costa Rica. Jackson was set on going to Iceland together and splashing around the Blue Lagoon and catching sight of the Northern Lights.

"We'll do it all together," he said, reaching across the table and squeezing my hand. I nodded, feeling blissful. Jackson wasn't full of empty words. He wasn't someone who spun a good sounding yarn for the sake of getting into a girl's pants. He was the first man I'd ever fully trusted. And what he said, I knew he meant.

We sat at the table, finishing our drinks as our plates were cleared, when Jackson reached into his pocket. He pulled out a small box, tied up with a silky purple ribbon. *Oh my god, he wasn't going to propose here, was he?*

He began to laugh as he saw the unmistakable shock cross my face. "Don't worry, it's not *that*." My shoulders relaxed and I let out a sigh as he handed me the box. "I just wanted to give you a little something to show you how much I adore you. And so you'd always have a little piece of me . . . sort of."

I untied the thin ribbon and opened the box. Inside was a delicate gold chain with a round moonstone pendant. The stone had a slight blue cast, shimmering and cool. As I held it up, I saw a thousand tiny rainbows hiding inside.

"Jackson, I — "I blinked back tears as I admired the necklace.

"It's a moonstone," he said. I met his gaze. His bright grey eyes were wide and shining as he smiled at me.

"I know, it's gorgeous. I've never . . ." I lost all words as I swiped at my cheek, brushing away a tear. I got up and sat myself in his lap, curling my arms around his neck and kissing him as deeply as I could. I tried to pour all the things I couldn't manage to verbalize into the kiss, the sweet hint of lime on my lips. God, I loved him so freaking' much. I didn't know I could ever feel something so overwhelming yet so totally right.

His fingers gripped my waist as he kissed me back. My heart was thundering inside my chest, drowning out the noise of the restaurant. He gently kissed my forehead before taking the necklace out of the box. Carefully, he placed the delicate chain around my neck. I fingered the cool moonstone, taking the moment in as I leaned against his chest.

"It's not too on the nose? A moonstone?" he asked.

"No. Not at all. It's perfect, Jack." I leaned in and kissed his soft lips again. I knew I would never tire of kissing them.

The waiter came with our check, pulling me out of my lovestruck daze. I blushed, still in Jackson's lap, and returned to my seat. Jackson threw down his card, smiling at me as the waiter whisked it away.

"Do you want to come upstate and meet my mom?" I blurted out, trying hard to drown out the rapid thunder of my heartbeat.

Jackson began to laugh, his grey eyes crinkling at the corners. "I'd love to, but you don't have to ask so aggressively," he teased.

"Ha. Ha." I rolled my eyes and, across the restaurant table, threaded my fingers through his.

"But really, Vi, I would love to see where you grew up and meet your mother." He gingerly tucked my hair behind my ear, letting his fingers linger against my skin.

"Good," I sighed. "And hopefully, she won't be too extra and scare you off."

"I can handle it. It'll be fun." He leaned in and gave me a reassuring peck on the lips.

We held hands as we walked back to Jackson's Bushwick loft. We stopped outside a bar blasting salsa music so he could give me a twirl. I laughed and we kissed as we continued on our way. I now knew why so many songs, poems, and films were written about love. And I understood why Hattie was preoccupied with finding it. There really wasn't any other feeling like it. It was the most potent drug on earth, and now I was addicted.

The loft was empty. The rest of the pack was out, enjoying their Friday night. I had a sneaking suspicion that Jackson had requested that. We made love twice. We were loud and uninhibited, letting our

7

bodies move and sound however they wanted. My skin hummed every time he touched it, and he made me cum so many times I felt my head might explode or I'd pass out. As the final release surged through my body, a sudden gust of wind rattled his bedroom window. It blew wide open as I screamed ecstatically with his final thrust.

We lay in bed, catching our breath as our limbs stayed entangled under the cotton sheets. "You know, I've been thinking we should get the coven and the pack together," Jackson said.

"Oh?" I hadn't expected this. I knew my girls liked Jackson and they got along with him, but I wasn't sure how they'd feel about his pack. Would the dynamics be totally thrown off if the pack were introduced to the mix?

"Yeah, I mean, I think it'd be nice to have our friends meet . . . don't you?"

"Um . . . yeah, I guess so?"

"Look, we don't have to yet. But I also don't want you keeping the pack at arm's length, Vi." He was so patient with me, but I could see it starting to wear on him.

"I love the pack, you know that."

"What's your hesitation then?" His grey eyes narrowed as he searched my face.

Sage. That was my hesitation. But I couldn't say that, of course. I'd done a good job keeping Jackson and Sage apart since she kissed me on that street corner a few weeks ago. I still didn't understand what it meant. I just wanted to lock that secret up in a safe little box under my bed, where nobody could find it.

"You're right. I'm being weird again," I said with a sigh.

"Hey, I love your weirdness . . . " He smiled to reassure me, but I could see some reticence in his eyes. "I just don't want to get shut out." I knew I wasn't really an open. I wanted to be better, it just wasn't easy for me.

"I love you, Jackson. All of this is just new to me . . ." He grabbed my hand and squeezed it, hard but tender. "But I don't want you to feel like I'm trying to keep you out."

"I know. It's new for me, too."

"Well, you have a lot less emotional damage than I do." I laughed even though it wasn't funny. His soft lips curled into a sad smile. I inhaled sharply, brushing aside any pity he may have for me, and held his hand.

"I love you, Violet," he said.

"I love you, too." I pulled him in closer, wrapping my arms around his torso and kissing his lips ever so gently. He held me tightly in his taut arms as I buried my face into his neck, huffing his scent like a drug. It was both familiar and intoxicating. His arms felt like the safest place I could ever be. If I never had to leave the confines of them, I would be a happy girl.

HATTIE FURROWED HER BROW, biting her lip as she scanned the backs of the tarot cards fanned out before her on the ink blue velvet draped over the coffee table. The candlelight flickered across her pale face as she considered her options. The smell of cinnamon and rosemary filled the air as Reina stood above a bubbling cauldron in the kitchen. She stirred it deliberately, making careful counterclockwise circles with a wooden spoon. Bianca stood next to her, crushing fresh lavender into tiny pieces. She sprinkled them into the brew, and Reina kept churning the potion.

"Hattie, do you usually stir it 33 times counter-clockwise?" asked Reina, her eyes trained on the cauldron. She was practicing a third eye opening elixir, one of Hattie's specialties.

"I actually do 33 and a half. And add the tiniest bit of mugwort. I found that makes it take effect faster," Hattie called back into the kitchen before turning back to study the tarot cards. She waved her hand across the cards, closing her eyes as she began to select, feeling her way to the cards that called to her. Gingerly, she pressed her index finger onto one card after another, sliding them away from the others until she had seven cards face down in front of her. She opened her big blue eyes and looked at me, expectant.

Sage placed a cork trivet on the coffee table next to the tarot, and Reina brought in the steaming cauldron. She gently set it atop the cork and Bianca ladled the herbal elixir into small porcelain teacups.

We each took one and drank it, careful not to scald our tongues. I closed my eyes and let the liquid trickle down my throat, warming me from the inside. My skin began to hum, hyper aware of the air around me. Behind my eyelids, purple and indigo began to swirl like a shimmering galaxy. I knew it was working its magic, fast, just like Hattie had said.

I opened my eyes and saw Hattie gazing at me, excited and anxious for me to read her tarot. "Ready?" she asked. "I'm ready! I hope it's good . . . " Oh, sweet, optimistic Hattie.

"Okay." I turned over the first card on her right. "The Lovers." Oh, so fitting. Hattie's face lit up. "You are in a good place to manifest love, right now. There's a good chance you will meet a new partner and start a relationship."

"Finally," she said with a sigh of relief.

"You need to step into that power and learn to enjoy the process, though. Look," I said, pointing to the two naked figures on the card. Why are the lovers *always* naked? I mean, *I guess* I spent a lot of my time with Jackson sans clothes. "The two lovers stand among verdant trees with an angel watching over them. Don't just rush through the dating process and skip getting to know your partner on a soul level."

"Yes," she said, nodding excitedly. "Big yes."

I couldn't help but smile at her girlish enthusiasm, always the foil to my Ice Queen ways. Though they had melted considerably since meeting Jackson I flipped over the second card. "King of Swords. An ambitious, driven, and serious man will enter your life. It looks as if your next lover," I said, letting my fingers graze the first card, "will be a disciplined, logical, and successful man."

"Ooooh," Hattie murmured.

"*But* he may be a little restrained and unemotional. He could even be too power-driven," I warned.

"Big Slytherin vibes," joked Bianca. Hattie rolled her eyes.

"Those aren't necessarily bad qualities," I explained. "But you will want to be careful. He could be wonderful and intellectual and all that good stuff, but you'll need to be wary of being manipulated or controlled. That's the main thing I see as being a potential downside here."

"Okay," Hattie said, studying the card. The King sat atop a stone throne, sword in hand, upright and proud. His face was stern and unyielding. She tapped the card impatiently.

"Three of Pentacles. Oooh, you're going to be recognized for your talents and hard work. This card bodes well for career success."

"A promotion?"

"Maybe, but I think more for your herbalism. You know you're *such* a gifted herbalist and intuitive healer, Hattie. This card could be the reassurance you need. Maybe start selling those tinctures part time. You could do really well."

"Yes, that would be so great, Hattie! I've been *trying* to tell you to take it more seriously. I know you're worried nobody is going to buy anything, but you already give away brews and elixirs for free whenever somebody is in need," said Reina. The other girls nodded along encouragingly.

"Yeah, maybe." Hattie shrugged, keeping her eyes trained on the next card. I knew she just wanted to hear about relationship potential and what was in store for her love life. Who cares about herbalism when true love was on the line?

The silence was almost tactile as I flipped over the fourth card. "Three of Cups," I said. "A time for celebration and abundance. Whatever you're putting your energy into, you'll have some success. And it's important you take the time to enjoy it and spend time with your loved ones."

Hattie nodded for me to keep going. I flipped over the next card. "Three of Swords."

Her face immediately fell. "No . . ." she groaned softly. A red heart stabbed with three swords underneath storm clouds was emblazoned on the card.

"I'm sorry, babe." I looked at her dejected face, apologetic. "There will be heartbreak and pain and betrayal. So that lover— that King of Swords— may not be your forever man. But the positive aspect of the Three of Swords— "

"God, what on earth could be positive about that?" Hattie asked, exasperated.

"The truth will be revealed and you'll be able to heal and move forward. You won't be trapped in something that isn't ultimately right for you."

Hattie pouted, staring down the cards like a petulant child.

"Maybe it was just your fear that called you to that card? Like you manifested it because you get so anxious about finding a partner?" offered Sage. I could tell she was trying to be helpful.

"Could be it." I shrugged. "Even with magic, the cards are never set in stone. It's not like they are guaranteed to tell the future. They pick up on your energies."

"True . . ." Hattie said quietly, her frown slowly dissipating.

"Hey, you had three Threes in a row . . ." said Reina, pointing at the cards. "That's kind of cool." Hattie just shrugged her shoulders and nodded her head to the next card.

I carefully turned it over, Hattie waiting with bated breath. "Five of Cups." She groaned. "This breakup will be a loss, of course— *if that is what actually happens*," I added quickly before Hattie completely fell apart. She looked almost on the brink of tears. Classic Hattie. "There will be disappointment and sadness, but you still have love in your life. You must not forget that when you are feeling low." I pointed to the cloaked, almost spectral figure on the card, mourning the three spilled cups before him. Two cups stood upright behind him. "See, he's crying over the loss of those three chalices, but completely ignoring the two full ones that are behind him. He has not actually lost everything."

"No matter how many breakups you go through, Hattie, you're always gonna have us," said Reina.

"Exactly," I said.

"And you better not forget it," teased Bianca.

"I know, I know," groaned Hattie. "But I just want this next relationship to be it. I'm so sick of being single. I want love and marriage and babies! I can't help it."

"I know you do, babe. It's not easy," said Sage empathetically. Despite all our encouragement, Hattie still looked pouty.

"Go ahead, the last one. Let's get this over with," she said, totally dejected. I stifled a laugh at her dramatics. Deep down, all of us witches are still just girls looking for love.

"The Tower." A card that always caused a reaction, it featured a burning tower, figures falling from it, as a storm raged in the background. With the appearance of that card, it felt like the air had been sucked out of the room.

"You've got to be kidding me," said Hattie, exasperated. Bianca started to giggle, which led to me snickering, and then everyone ended up laughing. We all fed off of each other, bent over in stitches, laughing until we started to cry.

"I can't—" Hattie began, trying to catch her breath and wiping away her tears. "Believe . . . this . . ." The laughter died down finally. "Go on, then."

"Welp, the great thing about the Tower is the fresh start. Sure, there's destruction and a collapse of your ideals, but in that, you can find enlightenment and start over again. You'll build a stronger foundation the next time around."

"Great," she said flatly. Reina snorted again.

"Maybe this wasn't the reading you were hoping for. But these were the cards you were dealt . . . and heartbreak happens to the best of us."

"Well said, Violet, you're so comforting and eloquent in times of trouble," teased Bianca.

"Ugh." Hattie exhaled loudly. "This *sucks.*"

"Hey, none of this may even happen," I said.

"Vi, you're our best tarot reader. When have you ever given a reading that wasn't accurate?" she said, trying to mask just how much the cards had rattled her.

"There's a first time for everything?"

Hattie rolled her eyes as Reina slung an arm around her shoulder and gave her a squeeze. "Everything will be just fine," Reina said, trying to reassure her.

"Yeah, that shitty finance guy Sword King or whoever he may be sucks anyways. You'll be better off without him," said Bianca.

"After he's crushed my heart, you mean?"

"Yeah, exactly."

CHAPTER TWO

Jackson decided Gabe's birthday party would be the perfect opportunity for the pack and coven to meet. I truly loved every member of his pack, and Gabe and his boyfriend, Desi, were no exception. Gabe was a talented sculptor and rugby player – the complete package. He'd been mated to Desi, a funny and ambitious actor, for years. They were always warm and welcoming and made me see what Jackson and I could have as mates. This whole "being mated" thing was a new concept for me, so I would take any pointers I could get. I mean, just having a boyfriend was a new concept for me. But when you add the intensity of lycanthropes' mating custom and physiology? That was a whole heap of pressure.

I was a little nervous, but Reina and Hattie had come over to our apartment to get ready with Bianca and me. Just like at the academy, we drank cheap wine and did each other's makeup, belting along to our favorite throwback songs. Sage said she would just meet us at the bar later, but didn't say why she wasn't coming to get ready. I shrugged it off . . . but hoped it had nothing to do with avoiding me.

We took a cab to The Tilted Hollow, a popular underground haunt, and arrived at a truly raucous scene. The bar was humming as we wove through clusters of hyped-up patrons. The pack held court from a cluster of tables in the back corner of the Hollow. A bundle of glittery balloons hovered over the wooden tables, covered in an array of half-drunk glasses. The girls of the pack— Malin, Athena, and Fiona— were talking animatedly with a few people I didn't recognize.

They all looked stunning. Malin's white-blonde hair was slicked back, making her look even *more* modelesque— if that was even possible. Athena's auburn hair was parted deeply to the side and cascaded down like an old Hollywood starlet. It made her look softer than her usual "I'm a tough girl" look. Jackson's little sister, Fiona, had the same thick light brown hair as Jack, but she'd tied hers up into two space buns atop her head. She had purple glitter on her cheek bones that sparkled as she tilted her head towards the crowd, catching my eye.

Fiona waved and smiled excitedly. "Hey girl!" I called out.

"You look HOT!" She yelled back.

I laughed before returning the compliment. I wasn't sure where Jackson was, but I waved to Gabe when I caught a glimpse of him. He strode over to us as we approached the tables. He was wearing neon yellow short shorts with a black mesh turtleneck that showed off his perfectly chiseled torso and arms. A sparkling pink "Birthday Queen" sash was slung across his body.

"You look *amazing*," I said, eyeing him up and down dramatically.

"Thank you," Gabe replied, as he twirled for me.

"Happy Birthday!" I gave him a hug, my arms barely wrapping around his thick, Adonis-like build.

"Introduce me to your posse!" Desi exclaimed, as he came up behind Gabe and kissed him on the cheek.

"Yes, we want to meet the girls!" Gabe said.

I called the girls over from the bar where they were waiting to order drinks. "Bianca, Hattie, and Reina, meet Gabe and Desi." They all exchanged hellos and the perfunctory repetition of names.

"You ladies are gorgina!" said Desi.

"Totally gorgeous," agreed Gabe before taking a long sip of his mojito.

Reina insisted she buy us a round of shots, to which the group cheered. I was following them to the bar when a pair of familiar hands squeezed my waist. I spun around to see Jackson's beautiful smiling face and grey eyes twinkling in the low light of the bar.

"Damn, girl," he said. "You look incredible." Desi had given the directive to wear something that made us feel *'sexy and forever 21, but not cheap like the store.'* I ended up deciding to wear a slinky long sleeve dress with the lowest back known to mankind. It was blood red and barely covered my ass.

I leaned into Jackson's warm chest and tilted my head up to meet his lips with a deep kiss. I was feeling myself and got a thrill when Jackson gave my ass a covert squeeze as we kissed.

We slowly parted, and I was able to take in his outfit: a tight-fitting Brooklyn Brewery tee that was worn at the collar and hem. It clung to him like a film, and I couldn't wait to peel it off later. I ran my hands along his shoulders as I admired him. His legs were encased in the tightest skinny jeans I'd ever seen. I began to laugh as I marveled at how on earth he could have wriggled his muscular legs into them.

"What!? Desi said 'sexy and 21 again!'" Jackson laughed.

"I think I can see the family jewels," I teased. Jackson smirked and shrugged.

"Shots!!" cried out Reina, as she came up behind me with a tray full of shot glasses and nudged us back towards Gabe and Desi. "Come on Jackie-boy, I need to see you DRINK!" I loved it when Reina's bossy side came out. Jackson chuckled as he flashed me an impish look. Bianca began handing out the shot glasses full of tequila as Hattie passed out lime wedges.

The rest of the pack had caught a whiff of the shots being passed out and shuffled over from the table. Once everyone had a tiny glass in hand, Reina raised hers in the air as if to toast, but instead prompted me. "Vi, take it away."

Everyone's eyes were on me now. "Thanks for

putting me on the spot, Rei. Um . . . to Gabe, the sexiest birthday boy I have ever laid eyes on!" Desi whooped and everyone cried out in celebration before tossing back their shots. A wave of winces and grunts ran through the group as the alcohol burned its way down our throats. "Now let's dance!" cried Fiona as she began to corral everyone to the dancefloor.

WE WERE REVELING on the dance floor, the pack and coven seamlessly intertwined in movement when Sage entered the bar hand-in-hand with Mariah, the petite blonde witch she'd been casually dating. I didn't know too much about Mariah— Sage hadn't led us to believe they were that serious— except that she worked with Jackson at Three of Cups, the underground coffee shop. Their faces were spread wide with glossy-eyed smiles as they drifted over to us.

"Hey," Sage said slowly as she gave me a limp hug. She was definitely stoned. I could smell the heady, dank aroma of kush on her clothes. Mariah giggled beside her as she nodded in greeting, seemingly unable to form words.

"Seems like you guys have been having fun," I said. They swayed in place, giggling like conspiratorial little children.

I motioned to the pack to come over. "This is Sage, everyone. And Mariah." The pack nodded and said hellos, garbled by the thumping beat of the sound system. Hattie, Bianca, and Reina were already twisting away to the music.

Jackson wrapped his arms around me from behind and rocked against me rhythmically. I tilted my face up towards his ear. "They're blazed," I said.

"Good for them," he laughed before kissing my neck playfully. Then he reached down and grabbed my hand for a twirl. He spun me around the dance-floor until I couldn't stop smiling and laughing. Dancing with Jackson felt like a carnival ride. His momentum moved through me and made me feel giddy and dizzy, my stomach almost in my throat.

The dance floor ebbed and flowed as people left and returned with drinks or slipped away for a covert make out session in a darkened corner of the bar. Malin's ash blonde bob was now artfully mussed from an encounter with a towering man who looked like he could be a professional basketball player. Sage and Mariah stayed glued to each other, playfully attached at the lips as they danced together in between swigs of the same beer. Even Athena seemed to be enjoying herself. She was sandwiched between Desi and Gabe as they all rocked their hips and waved their arms wildly. All three of them whooped loudly in time with the song. Fiona laughed as she watched them while she danced in a circle with Hattie, Reina, and Bianca. The four girls rotated and shimmied as if they were moving around an invisible maypole.

Jackson leaned in and whispered into my ear,

"You should join them, babe." I nodded and kissed him quickly before shuffling into the circle.

THE NIGHT WAS WANING and some of us had returned to the back tables to drink water and rest our feet. Dancing in heels wasn't light work. Jackson had his arm slumped over my shoulder as I nursed a glass of ice water. Malin had returned to kissing her giant suitor at the next table, while everyone else was still on the dancefloor. Bianca and Hattie sat across from us as Bianca was telling us all about her latest date with Derek the demonologist.

"And then he took me up to his roof—" Bianca was saying, when Sage and Mariah plopped down across the table.

"What a night," Sage sighed loudly. "Top notch. One for the books!"

"You were really tearing it up out there," Jackson said with a bemused smile.

"I didn't know *you* had moves, Jack," Mariah commented.

"Yeah, I have to keep them under wraps at work. It would be too much," he joked. Sage's green eyes flashed towards me. I held her gaze for a second and gave a half smile before looking away. It didn't have to be awkward, though. We were just friends who were dating people that happened to be coworkers. Why should that be awkward? It just sounded messier than it was, that's all. Nothing weird here.

Mariah was swaying in her seat to the music, her

eyes no doubt glazed over from the heady combination of weed and booze. "You know it's really cool how you all can still be friends and hang out together in a group," she mused.

"What do you mean?" asked Bianca. She looked at me with an arched eyebrow, bemused. Mariah was down the crossfaded rabbit hole it seemed.

"Well, just like, you know . . . Sage and Violet, and then now with me . . . and Jack . . . it's cool. Nobody is weird about it." *What the fuck, Mariah!* My stomach dropped as I glared at Sage, her eyes frozen wide like a deer caught in headlights. Bianca and Hattie stared at me and then at Sage, waiting for an explanation. Jackson shifted in his seat.

"What are you talking about?" Bianca asked impatiently.

"Just that Sage and Violet hooked up but can still be cool with each other and have their new partners around," Mariah said. She let out an awkward giggle as she took in everyone's agog expressions.

"What?" Jackson asked flatly.

"Jackson—." He removed his arm from my shoulder and turned towards me, his grey eyes searching my face.

"When did you hook up?"

The girls went silent, looking at me with eyes wide in a mix of discomfort and anticipation. I paused, my voice caught in my throat. My face was hot. Tears began to well in my eyes as I tried to figure out what to say and how to say it. I needed to fix this fast.

"Can we . . . talk outside?" I said finally, my voice shaky. Jackson quickly stood up and walked purposefully towards the bar's front door. His shoulders were square and tense as I followed him outside.

The air was cold, and I had forgotten my coat. I wrapped my arms around myself to keep me warm. I wished Jackson would just give me a hug, hold me, his body warm against mine.

Jackson's jaw clenched as he repeated emphatically, *"When did you hook up with Sage?"* Anger and confusion flickered in his eyes. "I need to know *when*."

"We didn't hook up," I croaked, blinking back tears. "We just kissed. She kissed me. That's all it was, just a stupid little kiss." Jackson's face was contorted as if trying to process this information and how upset and hurt he should be.

"Please tell me this was *before* we mated." He looked desperate for me to reassure him that it was long in the past. I couldn't lie to him, though.

"I'm sorry," I said softly as I shook my head. It was so hard to look at him.

"Why did she kiss you, Violet?"

"I don't know!" He stared at me, his face wounded. "I don't know . . . she said she needed to know what it was like to kiss me before it was too late," I said quietly. I couldn't bear to look at Jackson anymore. Heartbreak painted across his beautiful face. I concentrated on the dirty cracked sidewalk below my feet. Silence stretched out between us as an angry gust of wind howled down the block, raising the tiny stubbly hairs on my bare legs.

"Do you have feelings for her?" Jackson asked softly.

I looked up at him and shook my head no. His silver eyes were shining and wet. "I love you so much, Jackson."

He nodded slowly. "Why didn't you tell me?" I shrugged as tears fell down my cheeks.

My runny mascara began to blur my vision. "I didn't want to hurt you."

"Violet, it *hurts* me that you didn't tell me. If it didn't mean anything to you, why keep it a secret?"

"I don't know . . . I'm sorry." My chest heaved as I started to sob into the night. I wiped away thick, wet tears until my hands were stained with black mascara. Finally, Jackson gently wrapped his arms around me.

"It's okay," he said softly. How could he be so kind to me right now? He should be shouting at me or leaving the party in a fit of rage. This wasn't right; I nudged him away.

"No, it's *not* okay. I hurt you," I said, my voice wobbling.

"You don't deserve this, Jackson. I shook my head frantically. I didn't want him to be *this* understanding; I didn't deserve his compassion.

"I can't — I'm sorry." My heart was racing and my breathing jagged. Booze and panic coursed through my veins, making it hard to think straight. I needed to get out of there fast. I couldn't be around Jackson. Not like this.

I turned on my heel and ran as fast as I could down the block and around the corner. I sobbed uncontrollably. I had to bend over to catch my breath. I heaved into the night, feeling like I might wretch.

"Violet!" I heard Jackson call my name behind me. I didn't want to see him, didn't want to look him in the eye.

"Jackson— please—just leave me— alone," I said between craggy breaths. He shook his head as he reached me, kneeling down beside me.

"It's okay. Deep breaths, remember." He looked into my eyes and began to inhale and exhale deeply, encouraging me to do the same. I tried to match his breathing as my tears began to stop.

"I'm so sorry, Jackson. "I can't do this. I'm getting a cab and going home."

"Violet," he reached for my hand, but I pulled back and grabbed my phone to order a car.

"I'm sorry."

"Do you *really* want to go home alone right now?"

"Yes." The car service app had a grey sedan a block away. I kept my eyes trained on the corner, unable to look at Jackson anymore. If I did, I knew I'd give in and ask him to come home with me.

The car arrived quickly. I hopped in, muttering "I'm sorry" to Jackson. I didn't have the courage to meet his eyes. As the car pulled away, I glanced back. He stood

alone in the middle of the sidewalk, his face pale

and defeated. His shoulders slumped over as he looked down, burying his face in his hands in frustration. My breath wobbled as I quickly blinked, willing the tears to stop. I clutched at the moonstone dangling from my neck, cursing myself for being such a fool.

I should have known a love like that would never be for me. I couldn't trust myself with someone's heart. I'd just break it inevitably.

CHAPTER THREE

I woke the next morning, empty and upset. I wanted to cry, desperately. But the tears didn't come. They'd all already been cried out the night before. I had nothing left. Feeling parched, I rolled over and dragged my hungover body out of bed. I slipped my cold feet into my fuzzy slippers and opened the bedroom door.

Bianca was already awake and in the kitchen. She handed me a tall glass of water, ice cubes clinking. "Thought you might need this," she said. I nodded and began to chug until the glass was empty.

"Thanks," I croaked as I padded over to the sink and refilled it.

"I made breakfast for us," Bianca announced. I looked over at the little kitchen table. She'd made blueberry buttermilk pancakes, my absolute favorite. They looked fluffy and delicious. But my appetite had already left the building.

Bianca motioned for me to sit down with her, as

she poured the syrup over her stack in a methodical zigzag motion. I slouched into the chair across from her and curled my fingers around the mug of hot coffee. It was the color of salted caramel, milky and warm. I took a long sip, letting it slurp so I didn't burn my tongue. Despite everything, it was a perfect cup of coffee.

"Thanks for doing this, B," I said. She looked at me with her eyebrows arched in concern, her face tinged with pity. "What?"

"Vi, you *know* what. What happened last night? After the big reveal, you disappeared and Jackson came back to the bar and said a quick, *very* sullen goodbye and left." She speared a bite of pancake on her fork and brought it to her mouth as she studied my face.

"I think Jackson and I broke up."

"You *think* or you actually *did*?"

"I just . . . ran away from him after we talked. I left him standing there. I couldn't deal." I idly poked at my stack of pancakes, pushing them around my plate as if that might coax my hunger out of hiding.

"Oof," Bianca sighed. "So, you and Sage really hooked up then?"

"She kissed me. That's all," I said with a shrug, trying to brush off the memory of Sage's lips on mine. If I lingered on it for a moment too long, my skin would tingle, begging to be touched. I'd rather pretend it never happened and keep my coven and relationship free of messy feelings.

"*What?* When did she kiss you? And why didn't you tell me!?"

"A few weeks ago. Maybe a month . . . it's not like I kept track. It wasn't a big deal," I said. I didn't want to elaborate or admit to Bianca that I refused to keep track. It was a very active choice. I didn't want to stew in whatever I was feeling for Sage.

"*Violet.*" Bianca gave me that signature 'get real' look of hers, and I caved.

"Okay . . . yeah," I groaned. "It was weird."

"Do you have a thing for Sage?" Her eyes searched my face as she chewed a mouthful of pancake.

"No!" I paused. "I don't know . . ." I forced a bite of pancake into my mouth. A blueberry burst, juicy and tart as I chewed. You had to hand it to Bianca. They were really freaking good pancakes. I just wished I could enjoy them more.

"Okay . . ." Bianca nodded solemnly as she chewed. "And what about Jackson?"

"I *love* Jackson. But I also hurt him, and then I ran away . . . just like my dad did." I winced the minute it came out of my mouth. I felt so stupid saying it out loud. I sounded like a hurt little girl, and I hated that.

"Vi, people make mistakes." Bianca reached across the table and squeezed my hand, her warm brown eyes open wide, her expression soft and sweet. I began to cry. She got up from the table and wrapped her arms around me, letting me cry into her bleached and unruly mane of hair as she stroked my back. "It's gonna be okay," she said softly. I relaxed into her and let myself be held as I cried for what felt like the millionth time in the last twenty-four hours.

THAT AFTERNOON BIANCA and I lounged on the couch watching old episodes of *The Real Housewives of Beverly Hills* when the door buzzed loudly. It was a favorite of ours to watch when we were down or needed an escape from our lives. So much better to dive into their drama rather than our own.

"Did you order food?" I asked Bianca.

"Nope. Are you expecting any packages? Doing any heartbroken online shopping?"

"I don't think so," I said as I got up and went to the front door. I held down the button that connected with the voice box outside. "Hello? Who is it?"

"Vi, it's Jack."

I glanced at Bianca who paused the television, her attention on me instead. I guess my drama was better than Bravo.

"Well, let him in," she said, getting up from the couch. "I'll go to my room."

I buzzed him into the apartment building. I waited in our doorframe, listening to Jackson climb the stairs. A wave of anticipation rolled through my body. He rounded the corner, coming into view. His hair was damp from the afternoon drizzle.

"Hey," he said with a slight smile.

We hugged out of habit. But I nuzzled my face into Jackson's chest, trying to soak up every ounce of the feeling of being held by him. This could be the last time, and I wanted to remember it.

I led him inside and into my bedroom, quietly closing the door behind us. Jackson took off his shoes and jacket before joining me on the bed. We sat facing one another, each waiting for the other to speak first.

"I just wanted to make sure you were okay," Jackson offered. "After last night."

"Oh, I mean, I've been better." I picked at the pilled cuff of my sweatpants.

"I was worried about you."

"You shouldn't have been. I was *awful* to you."

"That's a bit extreme," Jackson said.

"I literally ran away from you," I said, still fiddling with my sweatpants.

"True, but it was just our first fight." He grabbed my hand and held it in his long fingers. I looked up at him. His silver eyes were so kind. It just made me feel more guilty.

"You say it as if there will be more of them . . ."

"There probably will be," he said as he squeezed my hand. He let out a small laugh. "Just don't run away next time and I think we will be fine." He was trying to tease me and make me feel better, but my stomach was sinking.

"Jack, I don't want there to be a next time. I couldn't bear it if I hurt you again. Or if I run away again when things get hard."

"Well, the hurt might be inevitable sometimes. We aren't perfect, but you're my mate, and I love you." He said it so plainly. It was just a fact to him. We were mated and we loved each other. As if that was enough. But I wasn't convinced it *was* enough. I had seen firsthand how love and commitment wasn't always everything you needed to withstand the disagreements and the pain. I'd weathered enough of my parents' fights growing up. I never wanted to risk being in that kind of a situation.

"Jackson, I love you *so* much. But I don't know if that's enough." He furrowed his brow as I blinked back tears. "I don't think I'm built for this, I'm sorry."

"Violet, c'mon, don't be so dramatic again," he sighed.

"I'm not being dramatic," I snapped. He wasn't listening to me. "I don't ever want to hurt you again. And it's just better if we both hurt now and deal with the pain because it will only be worse in the future. And I can't bear the thought of that . . ." I swiped at my cheek, brushing my tears aside. I didn't want to cry anymore; I was too tired.

"Violet, come here," Jackson said softly, drawing me into his arms. I let my weight fall into him as he held me close. "We can work through this. It's just a bump in the road."

"How can you be so nice to me right now?" I sniffled into his warm sweatshirt.

"It was one kiss. Sure, it sucks and I feel hurt, but I'm gonna get over it."

"So, say you get over it, but I fuck up again . . . then what?"

"Well for starters, don't kiss anyone else," he paused, gathering his thoughts. "But Violet, we're going to have our differences, and we're going to piss each other off sometimes and we'll fight and we'll get annoyed, but we will work through it. That's what relationships are."

"Which is exactly why I haven't been in any, and probably shouldn't be in any."

Jackson rolled his eyes and sighed. "You're being really difficult, you know that."

"Maybe . . ." I said. "But I promise, I'm just trying to protect you."

"Well, that's absurd. How many times do I have to tell you that I love you, Violet? When will you get that through that pretty skull of yours," he said with a frustrated little chuckle. "You're my mate. I see you as my future, and I'm not going anywhere."

I sighed and let him hold me in silence for a few minutes before finally pulling away and looking into his face. "You're too good to me, you know that." Jackson just shrugged. "I mean it!"

"I'm sure I'll do something to piss you off or hurt you at some point in the future, don't worry," he teased.

"I'll believe it when I see it," I let myself lean into him again. He laughed softly as he began to run his fingers through my hair.

Was this what love was? Forgiveness and choosing to run towards our issues together rather than running away . . . Carnal love came so much easier to me. I could touch and lick and kiss Jackson until I was drained of all physical energy. But he had this deep well of love I wasn't sure I'd ever experienced. A type of love I didn't understand. I hated that I had such a hard time accepting this, trusting it. Trusting *him*.

I curled into a fetal position as Jackson fixed his body around mine like a fortress, his body warm and protective. He buried his face into my hair and sighed. "I love you," he said quietly.

"I love you too. I'm sorry I tried to push you away," I said.

"I don't know what I'd do if I ever lost you, Vi." I wanted to be as sure and steady for him as he was able to be for me.

He began to trace his fingertips along my shoulders and down my arm. It tickled a little but felt good. He continued to repeat this motion, letting his hands skate down my body, eventually making their way to the indent of my waist and the pronounced curve of my hips. His fingertips trailed down my thigh and knee, sloping down to my ankle, before brushing back up and starting all over again. He traced the form of my body like an artist preparing his canvas. I let out a low purr as a craving for him began to stir inside me. It spread from the warm place between my legs into my stomach and over my breasts.

"*Jack*," I sighed, as he brushed my hair off of my neck and began to kiss the hollow space in my clavicle. His firm hand slid up under my shirt and began to tease my nipple. I began to rock my hips into his, and I could feel how stiff he was as he pushed himself against my backside. He grunted as I began swiveling my hips in a figure eight motion. He pinched my nipple, and a moan escaped my lips, spurring him on. I reached behind me and found the rigid angle of his hips and pulled him against me harder. He groaned in desire and my heartbeat dropped into my groin. My body was pulsating; I was desperate for him.

I rolled over to face him and kissed him hungrily, knotting my fingers through his thick hair. He peeled my clothes off, admiring me lustfully. His hands roamed my naked body greedily, grabbing every bit of flesh he could. I pulled his shirt off and ran my hands over his rippled chest, letting the tufts of chest hair fall through my fingers, before pushing his pants and boxers down over his hips and towards his ankles. He gave a little kick as they bunched up around his ankles, tossing them aside altogether.

We pushed our bodies against one another, feeling nothing but the warmth of each other's bare skin. He threaded one hand through my hair, grabbing a fistful and holding it tightly, making my scalp tingle, while his other hand slid between my thighs and began to curl into me. I gasped. He knew exactly how to touch me, how to make my body feel more alive and electric than it ever had before.

My body began to writhe as he swirled his fingertips and kissed my neck. My vision blurred as the sounds of my uncontrollable moans filled the air. "Yeah . . . yeah . . ." he murmured over and over in between kisses as my body undulated.

I desperately reached for him and began stroking

as my body began to undulate more frantically. He groaned as I gripped him.

"I need you inside me," I panted. "Jackson, I need you." Tears began to streak down my cheeks as the pressure inside me was mounting to a tipping point.

"*Violet*," he moaned as he plunged into me.

"Fuck," I gasped as I dug my fingernails into his back and bucked my hips against him. The air around us swirled like a vortex, encompassing our intertwined bodies.

"My sylph," Jackson laughed, as he brushed my hair out of my face as it whipped around in the wind.

"You know I can't help it," I panted.

"My wild woman— I love it." He thrusted faster as our breathing turned ragged and shallow. My moans mixed with his grunts in a rhythmic chorus in time with every thrust until we burst, my eyes seeing stars.

Our bodies slackened against each other as we lay there, catching our breaths. I looked up at Jackson's face, serene and slightly sweaty. He smiled and kissed my forehead before I rested it on his chest. He cradled his arm around me.

"I love you so much, Jack," I said into the silence. "And I don't know what I'd do either . . . if I ever lost you."

"You won't ever lose me, I promise." I sighed contentedly as his chest hair tickled my cheek.

CHAPTER FOUR

It was one of my favorite times of the year. The coven was gathering at Reina's and Hattie's for Ostara, the spring equinox. I was looking forward to a celebratory and boozy night with my girls. We were greeted at the door with warm hugs from Hattie. "Happy Vernal Equinox!" Hattie squealed as she ushered us inside.

Reina was already pouring us glasses of bubbly when we got to the kitchen. She handed me a flute. Without thinking, I downed the glass, carbonation almost getting lodged in my throat.

"Easy tiger," Reina joked as she poured more of that liquid gold into my glass.

"It's been a week," I said as I took a slower sip this time. "And I'm ready to party."

"Fair enough."

"Hey," Sage said as she came into the kitchen.

"Hey," I said, giving her a perfunctory half-hearted hug. "Happy Ostara."

"Happy Ostara," she said, raising her glass before taking a small sip. She paused, looking at me. "Are we okay?"

"Mhmm," I nodded. "Yep, we're okay." I did *not* want to talk about it. Especially here with everyone around. It had already been awkward enough everyone finding out about our kiss at Gabe's birthday party. *Time to move on and pretend it never happened.*

"Cool . . ." she trailed off. Thank god, she was willing to drop it.

I brought my glass to my lips and let the bubbles tickle my mouth and the tip of my nose. The apartment was flush with greenery. I looked around and admired all the work Hattie and Reina had put into the decorations for today. Vines trailed along the tops of the kitchen cabinets, and a verdant wreath adorned the door to the garden. A white ceramic vase filled with multicolored tulips in purples, oranges, yellows, and pinks sat atop the kitchen table. There was a potted plant at each seat along with a large brown speckled egg. The windows around the apartment were open, allowing a cool spring breeze to float through the space.

Ostara always made me a little nostalgic for being a kid. My mom would glom on conventional Easter activities to our celebrations. I'd get a stuffed bunny and chocolates and hunt for eggs that I'd painted the night before. We'd always spend a portion of the day tending to the garden out back, which she always told me was her favorite place in the world.

I loved watching her garden. Her raven hair would curl around her face and fall into her eyes as she bent over her herbs and daffodils and tulips and roses. She'd brush it out of the way, inevitably streaking her cheek with dirt. I had a little rainbow shovel I'd use to dig in an empty dirt bed when I was too little to actually help. As I got older, she'd shown me how she enchanted the plants and the tricks she used to prune them just perfectly.

That night after dinner, we sat on the worn wooden floors cross-legged in a circle, holding our eggs. One by one, we set them on the floor and focused our eyes on the brown speckled eggs. We held hands and meditated together as the eggs began to spin like tops, teetering on their bottom curves. Our collective energy kept the eggs delicately balanced as we began to speak into the circle what we wished to balance in our own lives.

"Being my own person and wanting a partner," said Hattie.

"Desire and practicality," said Bianca.

"My emotions being either too guarded and distant and or too overwhelming and confusing," I said.

"Giving too much to others and not enough to myself," said Sage.

"Learning moderation," said Reina.

We held each other's hopes for harmony and balance in our hearts as we continued to meditate in silence, our eggs slowing their spinning. Each egg was balanced perfectly on its rounded bottom until we ended the ritual with a thank you to our higher selves and one another.

Then we focused our attention on the small potted plants we'd been given by Hattie. Mine was a small lavender plant that had not yet bore any purple blooms. We each clasped our individual terracotta pots and began to recite an incantation for growth and fertility. I narrowed my eyes and focused all of my energy and desire on the small green shrub. It began to lengthen and sprout more delicate leaves until the narrow fragrant lavender buds began to unfurl and grow larger. Before my very eyes, the plant bloomed proudly. I exhaled slowly with a smile, admiring my work before bringing the pot to my face. I inhaled deeply, taking in the earthy, grounding scent of lavender. I felt my frayed nerves relax finally at that moment and felt incredibly grateful for magic.

AFTER OUR RITUALS, we celebrated Ostara with an impromptu dance party and Fleetwood Mac sing-a-long. Cliché? Sure, but witches gonna witch, I guess. I'd lost count of how many glasses of prosecco I'd had, but I knew it had been a *lot*. If I sat down and closed my eyes, I could feel the room spin like a tilt-a-whirl.

"Okay, I think I'm gonna have to cut you off, babe," Bianca said as she took my empty champagne flute out of my hand before I could pour myself another glass.

"Nooooo," I whined. "I want more!"

"Why don't we get some fresh air?" Sage said as she began steering me by the elbow towards the backyard.

"Fiiiiine," I groaned.

We settled onto a wooden bench at the back of the garden. I felt I needed to steady myself so I slouched against Sage's shoulder.

"Is this okay?" I asked, looking up at her green eyes. They looked deep and oceanic in the moonlight.

"Of course," she said as she slung her arm over me to help keep me propped up.

We sat in silence, taking in the sounds of the city at night. A distant siren wailed. Some people were smoking and talking in their backyard a few doors down, and snippets of their conversation floated by. Squirrels occasionally rustled in the trees overhead. I tried to focus on those little noises, to funnel my attention into them instead of the alcohol sloshing around inside me.

Sage began stroking my back soothingly. I leaned into her with more of my weight. "That feels nice," I said quietly. I rested my hand on her thigh and began tracing her knee absentmindedly as I sighed contentedly.

She shifted on the bench, so I sat back up and steadied my eyes on her pale face. It was as if her beautiful turquoise head was the only still object to which I could anchor myself.

"You okay?" she asked, her eyebrow arched in concern. I nodded. "I don't want things to be weird between us. I shouldn't have kissed you." A sobering chill ran over my body as she acknowledged our mistake.

"It's okay . . ." I didn't know what else to say.

Sage shrugged and stood up. "It's cold out here. I'm gonna head back inside." She strode through the garden back into the apartment. I felt compelled to follow her, but my body stayed affixed to the cold bench as my eyes reluctantly traced the curve of her hips as they swayed.

CHAPTER FIVE

That night the coven met for a lecture being given at Sage's store, Light and Shadow. Sage often hosted educational events like this to bring the underground community together and provide a free opportunity for people to learn and expand their knowledge. A prominent underground herbalist, Freida Troutman, would be talking about her new book while Sage facilitated a discussion with the audience at the shop after hours.

The attendees milled about afterward, sipping their wine and chatting. Some formed a line to have their book copies signed by Freida. The girls and I were huddled together with our wine glasses while Sage flitted between clusters of people, playing host. We were chatting about the event, when a man tapped Hattie on the shoulder. He was tall and lanky, with an angular face. His cheekbones and chin seemed to jut out from the rest of his body in a surprisingly handsome way.

"Excuse me." He had a vague accent I couldn't quite place. "I hope I'm not interrupting you ladies, but I had to introduce myself. I couldn't help but notice you during the talk." He looked down at Hattie, showing off a boyish grin.

"Oh, that's alright," she giggled, blushing pink. She smiled sweetly and reached out her hand delicately. "I'm Hattie. These are my girlfriends— Reina, Bianca, and Violet." He smiled and nodded at us as he shook her hand.

"I'm Casimir. It's lovely to meet you."

"What did you think of the talk?" Hattie asked.

"Fascinating. Were you familiar with Ms. Troutman's work?"

"Oh yes, I have all of her books," Hattie said with a smile, her pale blue eyes sparkling.

"Hattie's also a gifted herbalist," Reina interjected. Quick on the uptake, Reina was always game to play matchmaker.

"Oh, perhaps you could teach me a thing or two, then," Casimir said, flirting. I was impressed by how little time he wasted, and I could see Hattie was enjoying the attention. I might have found it creepy, but hey, different strokes for different folks.

"Perhaps I could," Hattie said girlishly, before taking another sip of wine. Bianca flashed Reina and me a knowing grin, raising an eyebrow. I bit my lip, stifling a giggle.

"I'm gonna go see if Sage needs help," I said, politely excusing myself.

"Oh, we'll go with you," Bianca added, grabbing onto Reina's elbow. Very smooth.

"Lovely to meet you, Casimir," I said as the three of us turned away and started to giggle like schoolgirls.

"Have you ever seen him around here before?" I asked the two of them just out of earshot, eager for the drama.

"No, I don't recognize him," said Bianca.

"Maybe he doesn't live in Brooklyn," guessed Reina. We snaked our way through the groups of people chatting till we found Sage. She excused herself politely from a pair of redheaded identical twin sisters.

"Are those the Vogel sisters?" asked Reina.

"Yep," Sage nodded. The Vogel sisters were some of the first witches to begin using social media to their benefit. They were now influencers with over a million followers each, and those followers weren't just members of the underground. They had capitalized on the witchy new age trends in pop culture early enough to make a killing. Little did their followers know, these new moon manifestation rituals were real magic, not just a fun activity to make you *feel* witchy.

"Wow," murmured Reina, her eyes trained on them as they both moved to grab a glass of wine in perfect unison. Every movement they made was totally in sync, like they were each other's shadows. It was part of their brand, you could say.

We were about to tell Sage about Hattie's new

suitor when a striking woman with beautiful dark skin approached us.

"Wonderful evening. I'm Adeline," she said as she reached out her hand to Sage. A pair of gold bangles clinked on her wrist.

"Oh, thank you so much for coming. I'm Sage, the owner of the shop." Sage shook the woman's hand. She smiled proudly, and I could see just how confident she was in this moment. Sage was in her element in the shop; it was like a bright white light radiated from her when she was working.

"I know," said Adeline with a small smile. Sage nodded and introduced the rest of us.

"Do you live in the neighborhood?" I asked. She shook her head no and took a sip of her wine, blood red drops lingering on her lips. Her movements were regal and fluid, as if she was in a ballet.

"I'm in Brooklyn Heights," she said.

"Oh wow, that's adult Brooklyn," joked Bianca.

"Yes, it can be rather quiet sometimes," Adeline smiled politely. "You all should come over for drinks on the patio sometime. My coven and I are new in town."

"That sounds lovely," Reina said. Bianca and I nodded.

"We'd love to," I agreed.

"Fantastic. Let me get one of your numbers."

"Okay," Bianca said as Adeline handed her phone over so she could enter her contact details.

"Thanks," Adeline said as she slipped her phone back into her slim Chanel quilted purse. It was in pristine condition, not a scratch or smudge on the leather. I wondered if it was new or if she was just the kind of person who could own nice things and actually take good care of them.

"Are you girls a coven?" She asked as she caught me eyeing her bag. I tried not to blush and looked away.

"We are," said Bianca.

"And so is that girl over there," said Reina, pointing towards Hattie who was laughing at something Casimir had said to her. His hand grazed the small of her back as he leaned into her ear whispering something. We could all see Hattie was beaming.

"Oh, she's talking with Cas," Adeline said. "He's in my coven. We all moved here from Montreal not too long ago."

"Oh, what brought you all here?" Bianca asked.

"We needed a change of scenery," she said curtly, ending the conversation. Adeline's honey-colored eyes shifted focus as she began to scan the room. Her phone began to buzz from within her purse. She pulled it out and glanced at it before tossing it back inside. "Excuse me, I must be going," she said. "Thank you again for the lovely evening," she said before striding over to Casimir. She leaned into his ear and said something. He nodded and then kissed Hattie on both cheeks before leaving with Adeline. I wondered why they had to rush out so quickly, maybe they were headed to some fabulous Brooklyn Heights dinner party.

Hattie rushed over to us, her face excited and rosy. "I've got a date!"

"Congrats," said Reina. "He was really into you." Hattie nodded eagerly.

"And his friend Adeline invited us over for drinks sometime soon," said Sage. "I've got to make sure this Cas guy is good enough for our Hattie."

"Yeah, we've gotta make sure he's in it for the right reasons," agreed Bianca teasingly. Hattie rolled her eyes, but her smile didn't leave her face. She was glowing with that first hit of infatuation. It made me think of my first date with Jackson. All that excitement shimmering in the air.

"He's so cute, guys. I don't want to mess it up," Hattie said, her eyes wide.

"Hattie, there is nothing you could do to mess it up. If this dude doesn't see how amazing you are, it's his loss," I said.

"Yeah, seriously. Just be yourself and if it's meant to be, it will be," said Reina as the rest of us agreed.

"Okay, yeah, you're right," sighed Hattie, but she still looked a little unconvinced. "But what about the King of Swords? What if he's it?"

"Be careful, just protect your heart . . . and don't think too hard about it. It could just be a fun date!" I said.

"But the Three of Swords . . . the Tower . . . all the heartbreak and disappointment?" Hattie looked at me, her eyes large and pleading. I couldn't take away her fear, it was understandable, but I hated that she was already so worried about a guy she *just* met.

"I know, babe." I grabbed her tiny hand and gave it a squeeze, trying to assuage her anxiety. "Just try and have fun with it. It's just a date, remember." She nodded and relaxed a little, but I knew her mind was probably still racing. Typical Hattie.

"How are you and Jackson, by the way?" asked Reina, shifting the attention to me.

"We're good. He's way too understanding," I joked.

"You know that's a good thing, right?" said Bianca with a slight eye roll.

"Yeah, yeah, I know. I'm just not used to it," I shrugged.

"You know, Mariah was saying we should go on a double date," said Sage.

"Huh?" I asked. Why on earth would we go on a double date after our regretful kiss?

"You know, because she and Jackson work together and are kinda friends. She thought maybe it would smooth everything over if we just hang out."

"I thought everything was good," I said a little too defensively.

"We don't have to go," Sage laughed.

"No, no . . . a double date would be fine. I guess." I guess I could take the high road and be mature . . . even though every fiber of my being was screaming *"hell no."*

"Good, because I think Mariah already talked to Jackson about it earlier today at work."

"Really?" The girls all shifted on their feet awkwardly as Sage and I stared each other down.

"Yep, and Mo said he was game, so . . ."

"Oh, that's great, then. We can totally double date."

"Good."

"Great."

"Alright, well this has been sufficiently weird. I'm calling it a night, ladies," said Bianca. I nodded and said goodbye to the rest of the girls with Bianca before we headed home. Sage and I gave each other a halfhearted hug before leaving.

The minute we left the shop, Bianca blurted out, "What the hell was that? That was tense as fuck."

"I have no idea."

"Well, I don't know what is going on between you two but you need to sort it out. Don't let this fuck up the coven, Vi. Go on the awkward ass double date if you have to, just make things good between you and Sage."

"Okay, I will." I nodded solemnly, silently cursing the mess I'd found myself in. The last thing I wanted to do was be stuck on a date with Jackson and Sage pretending like that kiss had never happened.

CHAPTER SIX

"And you sure you're okay with this?" I asked Jackson for the umpteenth time as we approached the restaurant.

"Yes, Violet. I am very much okay with this. Mariah was really excited about it."

"And you won't be weird around Sage?"

"No, it will be fine, babe." He squeezed my hand and smiled at me reassuringly.

"Okay," I sighed. "Sorry, I just think this whole thing is kind of weird."

"Yeah, maybe," Jack shrugged. "But whatever, they're both cool girls. We can all be friends."

"God, you're so chill. *Too* chill. I need to be more like you."

Jackson laughed as he pulled the door to the little Italian restaurant open for me. Sage and Mariah were already seated inside. Mariah waved and Sage smiled as they spotted us.

"Hello, hello," said Jackson as he slid into the booth.

"Hey," I said, watching Sage and Mariah.

"Hi!" trilled Mariah. "Jack, I think you're really gonna love this spot. Their Bolognese is bomb."

"Mo has been talking it up all day," Sage said as she rested her hand on top of Mariah's. They had matching dark purple metallic nail polish. I glanced down at my bare nails, feeling inadequate. Who cares if they wanted to wear the same nail polish color? Sage caught me eyeing their hands and added, "Did you work today, Vi?"

I shifted awkwardly in the booth. "Yeah, it was a pretty busy morning. How's the shop?"

"Also busy," she said. Well, this was certainly civil.

Mariah started to giggle. I looked at her and she shrugged. "Sorry, guys, this is just *so* awkward."

"Agreed," I said.

"It really doesn't need to be, though," Sage insisted. "Jackson, I hope you aren't uncomfortable. I really do appreciate you coming." Was this her being a bigger person? Mature and communicative, whereas I just wanted to fake diarrhea and leave ASAP.

"Thanks, Sage. I mean, it's weird, I guess, but we're going to be in each other's lives. Violet's my mate and you're in the same coven, so . . ." Jackson raised his eyebrows and tilted his head as if to say *what can you do?*

"Great! We can all just move forward and be friends," said Mariah.

"Yeah," agreed Sage, smiling at Mariah. There was a familiar glint in her green eyes as she watched Mariah talk. It made my chest tight. No matter what Mariah said, this did *not* feel cool.

"Sounds good to me," Jackson said as he gave my thigh a squeeze under the table. I fought the urge to roll my eyes. Why was I getting so annoyed? Everybody was just acting normal. Sage and I had kissed only a month or two earlier — that's weird, right? How could they all be so understanding and calm about it all? It irked me. They should be snapping at me, or at least icing me out. Let me sit in my misery and guilt, people! I deserved that.

Sage ordered a bottle of sangiovese for the table while Mariah and Jackson told funny stories about some of their most eccentric regulars at Three of Cups. I piped in every once in a while, but spent the evening quieter than usual.

When Sage and Mariah got up to go to the bathroom, Jackson leaned into me. "Are you ok?"

"Yeah, I'm just tired," I said. He nodded but I could tell he wasn't convinced.

We all ended up getting the Bolognese on Mariah's recommendation. And it was indeed, bomb— succulent and meaty, with carrots, tomatoes, and onions. At least I was getting a good meal out of this night.

"You were so right, Mo-bear," said Sage between mouthfuls of pasta. *Mo-bear?*

"I knew you'd love it," smiled Mariah. She looked up at Sage so happily, I realized I needed to stop being salty. I wasn't even sure *why* I was bothered. I was in my own relationship with Jackson, whom I loved completely. And Sage and Mariah seemed to really like each other. Whatever she had felt for me seemed to have dissipated— which was good, right?

THAT NIGHT I SLEPT RESTLESSLY, slick with sweat and damp covers tangled around my body. I dreamed I was with Sage that night and not Jackson. I guided her towards the bed, never letting my lips leave hers. She twisted me around and pushed me onto the bed, pressing her body into mine. I kissed her harder and our bodies began undulating against each other, as if floating in the ocean.

I ran my hands down her back until I found her pert behind and gave it a squeeze. She murmured excitedly as she ran her fingers down my torso and began peeling my top up over my breasts. She pulled my bralette down and began to trace her tongue down my neck and then stomach.

Dream Sage undid my jeans, tugged them off and tossed them aside before caressing me. She kissed the thin lace of my underwear before pulling it aside and teasing me with her mouth. We both moaned as she explored my body. My back arched as the excitement surged through my body uncontrollably. I began to feel wild and untamed as she sucked and nibbled more fervently. My hips began to buck against her.

She grabbed them firmly and steadied me as she pressed her mouth harder against me, bringing me to orgasm. I gasped loudly, both in the dream but also in real life, waking myself suddenly.

I was short of breath and sweaty. Jackson was sleeping soundly next to me, his slow, deep breaths punctuating the silence. I felt a pang of guilt. Why couldn't I get Sage out of my head? Sure, I couldn't control my dreams, but I didn't want to be thinking of her like that. I knew I loved Jackson, but now I just felt more confused than ever. I wish Sage had never kissed me on that street corner. I didn't want to know how soft her lips felt against mine, or how warm and sure her hands felt as they gripped my waist. *Ugh.*

Quietly, I slipped out of bed, taking care not to rouse Jackson. His face looked so serene as he slept. I was tempted to run a finger along the crooked bridge of his nose, but didn't want to risk waking him. Instead, I padded into the kitchen and grabbed a glass of water. I drank fast, refilling it only to empty it once more. As I stood at the kitchen sink, I felt a pair of well-muscled arms wrap around my waist. I nearly jumped, but, surprisingly, they steadied me. My heart was still beating hard from my dream about Sage. "It's just me," whispered Jackson's familiar baritone voice.

I spun around to face him, and he smiled sleepily. His thick hair was sticking out adorably at messy angles. I reached up and ran my fingers through it, smoothing it down as scratched his scalp gently. He closed his eyes blissfully and I could see the wolf inside him as he practically purred while I pet him. I giggled softly, and he opened his eyes.

"Every touch of yours, Violet . . ." he trailed off and leaned in, his sleepy energy suddenly dissipating. He kissed me hungrily, taking me aback. I melted into him as he hooked one arm around my hips and lifted me onto the kitchen counter. I pulled him to me as I wrapped my legs around him. His boxers were already tented; he was ready to spring free. I reached for him— all thoughts of Sage had long dissipated— and tugged his boxers off, letting them fall to the floor.

He pulled my oversized T-shirt up over my hips, letting the fabric gather in their creases. I knotted my fingers through his bed head as we kissed, his low groans reverberating through me. I began to stroke him and moaned in anticipation. He caught my lip in his teeth and pulled gently. I needed him *now*. He grunted as I grabbed his behind, steering him into me. As he slid inside, we both sighed. His hands dug into my thighs, steadying me as he pushed into me. I could feel the warmth of him filling me and spreading throughout my body like syrup.

"You feel so good," I moaned. He kissed me harder, running his hands up under my shirt and grasping my breasts greedily.

"Violet, your body . . . I never want to stop . . ." he grunted in between kisses.

"Don't ever stop," I murmured as he thrust deeper.

"I won't," he bit out. "You're my mate. You are

mine, and I am yours. Forever." He was slick with sweat and panting. I pressed my hands into his ass and held him inside me, letting my hips do the rocking.

"Forever," I repeated breathlessly as I ground my hips against him faster. He groaned as my body began to writhe. He pinched my nipples, sending a jolt of electricity down my belly, before gliding his hands down to meet mine. He pulled them off his ass and held them firmly against the kitchen counter, taking over the thrusting. I gasped in ecstasy as he thrust into me, harder and faster until I was fighting back screams as pressure and pleasure rippled through my body as we both came in unison.

He collapsed, sweaty and tired, onto me as we caught our breath. I ran my fingers up and down his damp back, while the smell of sex lingered in the air. Nuzzling into my neck, he mumbled, "I love you," and kissed my shoulder.

"I love you, too," I said, smiling in the dark kitchen as the sounds of Brooklyn echoed in the far distance.

CHAPTER SEVEN

The five of us— Bianca, Reina, Hattie, Sage, and me— ascended the stoop of Casimir's and Adeline's towering old brownstone in Brooklyn Heights. He'd invited us over via Hattie for cocktails, one coven to another. We whispered excitedly as we noted the pristine attention to detail of the beautiful architecture. Classic old New York, unlike anywhere else in the world. The building was elegant and grand, looming over us like a brick castle. Brooklyn Heights was a swanky, historical neighborhood that abutted the East River and boasted breathtaking views of lower Manhattan and the Brooklyn Bridge. Many of the houses, including this brownstone by the looks of it, had been built in the 1800s.

"I read online this house was valued at 6.25 mill," said Bianca in a hushed voice. Zillowing local real estate was a favorite pastime of ours. Comparing rents was our nosy version of asking about jobs or hometowns. "What do they do again?" asked Reina.

"It wasn't entirely clear," said Hattie.

"Huh," murmured Sage, as she eyed the small security camera that hung above the arched front door.

"Just be cool, okay?" Hattie said nervously as she rang the doorbell.

"Yes, we will be on our coolest behavior for your new boyfriend," I smirked.

"I just met him!" sighed Hattie as she shifted her weight back and forth. Her eyes stayed focused on the wooden front door. Bianca and Reina stifled giggles.

The door swung open, revealing Adeline smiling and draped in a flowy silk kaftan and bare feet. Her dark toes were painted an emerald green. She looked like the epitome of a rich socialite. "Welcome!" she exclaimed, spreading her arms wide. We filed in one by one, each of us exchanging the customary kiss-kiss on the cheeks as if we were walking through the receiving line of a wedding reception.

"I'm so glad you ladies could make it," Adeline said as she led us through the main floor of the house and into the back sitting room. Its tall windows looked out onto a small landscaped garden and patio. Casimir stood over a brass bar cart, mixing drinks. He looked up and beamed when he saw Hattie.

"Hello, hello," he said with a devilish grin. "Hope you all like Boulevardiers."

"Of course," said Hattie. I glanced at Bianca who shrugged.

"Remind me which one that is again," I said.

"Bourbon, Campari, and sweet vermouth," Casimir said as he winked at Hattie.

"Woof," I said. Adeline and Casimir chuckled. I'm sure I seemed totally unrefined to them.

"Sounds boozy, and I like boozy," said Reina.

"Amen," came a voice from behind us.

We all turned around to see a woman leaning against the carved wood molding of the room's entry. She had a striking black bob and wore long, flowy pants in a loud print that featured jewel-toned jaguars across it. Yet another look that screamed wealthy, well-to-do woman— not Brooklyn twenty-something like me and my girls. I tugged at my black denim miniskirt absentmindedly as I took her in. It had looked so cute in the mirror at home, but now I just felt underdressed and juvenile.

"I'm Nikki," she said. Her voice was low and buttery. I could imagine her singing jazz at a club in the West Village. She was the kind of witch whose aura you could practically feel radiating from her skin. Her magic must be seriously powerful.

"Hi, I'm Sage-"

"Yes, Sage, Reina, Hattie, Bianca, and Violet," she said as she nodded her head in our direction. She already knew who each of us was, and I saw a self-satisfied smile creep across her face.

"Quit showing off," said Adeline as she plopped onto the white couch. "Clairvoyant," she explained further before taking a sip of her cocktail.

We all nodded in understanding as Nikki

shrugged and said, "Guilty." She strode across the room and grabbed a Boulevardier from Casimir.

"So, what exactly brought you three to Brooklyn? Like why leave Montreal? It's such a great city," said Reina.

"And the healthcare is free," I added. Even us witches need modern medicine sometimes.

"Ah, well, I think we'd all kind of hit a wall," said Adeline.

"Yeah, it had become stagnant," said Nikki. "It wasn't as exciting as it had once been."

"And who doesn't want to live in New York City?" Casimir said, taking a sip of his Boulevardier. "You know what they say, if you can make it here, you can make it anywhere." I fought the urge to roll my eyes. I glanced at Hattie. She was clearly charmed, a genuine smile plastered across her face. I envied her lack of cynicism.

"And what do you all do?" asked Bianca, as she looked at each of them intently. They were all so poised, in beautiful expensive clothes. I wasn't sure how old they were, but they had to be at least ten years older than us. Even if they were in their mid-to-late thirties and rented the brownstone, living in this kind of a house was impressive. And it did not come cheap. Unfortunately, there is no spell or incantation that makes money appear out of thin air. We still have to abide by the mortal rules of capitalism.

"I'm a designer," said Adeline.

"And I'm an art dealer and part-time collector," said Casimir.

"And I'm a private chef," said Nikki.

"Wow, you're a talented coven," remarked Sage.

"Aw, that's very sweet to say," said Adeline. "We've all been blessed. And lucky."

"What about you ladies, what do you do? I already know Hattie is a gifted herbalist." Casimir gave Hattie's knee a squeeze and she smiled.

"I mean, I still work at a plant shop . . . hopefully at some point, I can be a healer or herbalist full time," said Hattie humbly. She never liked to boast, but Hattie was talented enough to practice herbalism for a living.

"I run Light and Shadow, that you already all know, I think," said Sage. Adeline, Nikki, and Casimir all smiled.

"What about you, Bianca?" asked Adeline.

"I'm a copywriter for a sex toy company," Bianca said nonchalantly. She flashed a red-lipped confident smile.

"Very cool," said Nikki.

The Trio looked at me expectantly. "I work at a bakery. I'm still trying to figure out what I want to do though," I said plainly. They all smiled politely.

"And you, Reina?" asked Adeline.

"I'm building my medium business, so I do that part-time and then dog-sit to make extra cash."

"She's an incredibly gifted medium," bragged Sage. Reina shrugged with a charming smile as if to say *guilty as charged*.

"I'm sure that could end up being quite lucrative

for you," said Casimir. "If you need a marketing person, I could give you some contacts."

"Oh, that would be great! I don't know if I'm there yet, but I would definitely take a look, thanks," Reina said.

I shifted in my seat as I watched everyone smiling superficially and sipping their cocktails. "Um, where's your restroom?" I asked.

"Just up the stairs, on the left," said Nikki.

"I'll join you," said Bianca, getting up and following me to the staircase in the front of the house. We wound our way up the stairs, quietly slipping past the guest bathroom. The stairs were slick and smooth, as if they'd just been polished. I wondered when they'd moved in. Everything seemed so perfectly clean.

Bianca waved to me, indicating silently that we should go all the way to the third floor. I followed her lead and when we landed on the top floor, we were greeted by a large circular stained-glass window. A ray of light from the lowering sun shimmered through the colorful glass and danced across the wooden floorboards. Together, we tiptoed across the small alcove to admire it up close, ignoring the two doors that flanked the landing.

Underneath the window, sat a narrow marble pedestal. Atop what looked to be a jagged quartz dagger with a gold hilt glinted in the streaming sunlight. It rested ceremoniously on a thin gold stand, as if displayed in a museum. I was surprised it wasn't protected behind glass. I'd never seen anything like it before. Somehow, it managed to look both angelic and demonic in equal measure.

"Whose do you think that is?" I asked, keeping my voice low.

"I don't know." Bianca reached out a finger to gently to touch the dagger.

"Don't touch that!" cried out a voice behind us. We spun around. Adeline stood at the top of the steps, glaring at us with eyes wide and jaw clenched. Then, as if she hadn't just screamed at us, she contorted her face into a smile. It was all too forced and unnerving. A chill ran down my spine, causing the peach fuzz on my arms to stand on end.

"I'm sorry, we were just looking around," said Bianca.

"You have such a beautiful home, we couldn't help it," I added.

"I understand." Adeline nodded with that tight-lipped smile. "It's just . . . that is a precious family heirloom, that dagger. I didn't mean to yell."

"Oh, it's okay. I get it," Bianca said. I could feel her body relax next to mine as we followed Adeline back downstairs.

"Why don't we all play some cards or something," Adeline offered as she rounded the corner of the stairs onto the next flight. "Wouldn't that be fun?"

"Sure," I said as I glanced at Bianca. She looked at me befuddled and silently mouthed the word *cards*. I couldn't put my finger on it, but something with Adeline was definitely off. I didn't know anything about cards, unless they were tarot. But I was game if it would ease the tension that had just developed in the last few minutes.

ON THE G train back to Greenpoint, Hattie gushed about Casimir and their new, budding romance. "He wants to take me out to Montauk this summer," she said excitedly. "One of his clients offered their beach house for a week in July."

"Are we invited?" Reina joked.

"What if this is really it?" asked Hattie, ignoring the question. "Cas could be my person." I wanted to tease her and say something like *barf*, but I was acutely aware that I was only a few degrees away from Hattie. Jackson and I had fallen hard and fast, and now I was in such a happy, loving relationship. Hattie deserved to find that, too. We all did.

"Just be careful," warned Sage. That surprised me. It wasn't like her to be a Debbie downer.

"What do you mean?" asked Hattie, a hint of defensiveness in her voice.

"I don't know . . . just protect your heart, that's all." Sage glanced at me, and I caught myself staring at her heart-shaped mouth for a second too long.

"I second that," said Bianca. She'd been quiet the whole ride so far. We all turned our attention to her. "What?"

"You're not telling us something," said Reina.

"I just got a weird vibe from them," said Bianca.

She flashed her cat-eye-lined brown eyes at me for reassurance. "Didn't you, Vi?"

"You mean the dagger thing?" I asked.

"Dagger thing?" asked Sage. "What dagger thing?"

"Yeah, there was this crystal dagger, like made of quartz or something, upstairs. Adeline caught us admiring it and kind of freaked out," I said.

"It was *so* strange," said Bianca. "Something was definitely off . . ."

"Maybe she was just upset you went snooping," said Hattie.

"How could you *not* in that house?" said Reina. "I don't blame you."

Hattie's round eyes searched for reassurance from us. "It doesn't sound like that has anything to do with Cas, though. He wasn't the one freaking out on you two." I was about to tell her she was right and that it was probably just Adeline being weird, when Bianca doubled down.

"I don't know, Hattie. There's something *different* about those three."

"Yeah, and how do they even afford that place? They're only, what? A decade older than us? At most?" said Sage.

Hattie looked at me and Reina. I shrugged, unsure what to say. Sure, they all seemed a bit strange, but I had no business getting involved. I had to be supportive of Hattie, especially after my own whirlwind romance. Hattie had been a great friend despite our breakneck pace and my hasty mating with Jackson.

Reina piped up. "They have a point, babe. Didn't it feel a little too . . . polished? Like they were putting on a performance almost."

"A really good performance," I said. The other girls nodded. Hattie looked disappointed. *Ugh.* "Hattie, I'm sure it will be fine. Cas clearly likes you. Just take your time in getting to know him." Hattie nodded, appreciative, and I felt a pang of guilt. I knew I didn't fully believe my own words, but I couldn't stand the sight of Hattie looking so dejected. And maybe everything *would* be okay.

CHAPTER EIGHT

I woke up curled next to Jackson, who had come over after his shift the night before. I could see he was already awake, reading the New York Times on his phone. "Morning, sleepyhead," he said, setting down the phone on the nightstand. He turned onto his side to face me before gingerly tucking a strand of hair behind my ear. "You were talking in your sleep."

"I was?"

He nodded. "Something about Hattie and a dagger."

"Oh." I paused, thinking about last night. It left a strange feeling in my chest. "Something weird happened at that coven's house yesterday. One of the women— Adeline— caught me and Bianca looking at this crystal dagger that was on display upstairs."

"What do you mean 'caught'?"

"Well . . . we kind of snuck upstairs to see the rest of the house. I mean, it's this *gorgeous* brownstone so we were curious. Fancier than anywhere I'll ever live.

She just happened to catch us as we were discovering this weird dagger that she ended up calling a 'precious family heirloom.'"

Jackson furrowed his brow. "What kind of family heirloom is a dagger? Were her ancestors ancient Roman assassins?" he joked. "But in all seriousness, that *is* strange."

"Yeah, it was so weird. The whole vibe of the night kind of shifted . . . there's just *something* about those three that I don't trust, but I can't put my finger on it."

"And Hattie is into the guy?"

"Oh, she's already fallen so hard, absolutely smitten."

"You think he's a bad dude?"

"I don't know if I'd say he's not a good person, just a little . . . too charismatic? Or put together? I don't know. Just seems like he's trying to move too fast."

"You know, we moved pretty fast ourselves."

"I know," I said, as I played with a tuft of his tawny chest hair. "But you're *you*. There's no way this guy is anything like you."

"I'm one of a kind, baby," he smiled at me playfully.

"You are!" I leaned in and gave him a sweet peck on the lips. "Plus, you're a lycanthrope. It's different."

"That's true. We wolves move fast," he said, squeezing my waist with his hand, with a goofy little growl. I giggled as he pulled me into him, the covers tangled around us as we kissed.

HATTIE'S cherubic face was flushed and beaming as she entered the apartment, unwinding her scarf from around her neck. "Sorry, I'm late," she said. "I got caught up at Cas's."

"Did you now?" asked Bianca with a sly smile.

Hattie looked sheepish, but then burst into a grin. "Yes, we spent the afternoon in bed. It was *very* romantic." Bianca and Reina began to coo, winding Hattie up. She rolled her eyes but her smile stayed put.

"It's only been what? A week?" I asked.

"A week and *a half*," Hattie sighed.

"Think you should slow down a bit?" I tried to be gentle with my question.

She swiveled her head around and snapped, "Did you and Jackson slow down?"

Bianca inhaled sharply and looked at me. Hattie was right, of course. We fell hard and fast for each other. But why wasn't I giving Hattie the same benefit of the doubt?

"I'm sorry," Hattie said, her face softening. She could never stay mad for long. "I shouldn't have said that."

"No, it's fair . . . you can move at whatever pace you want to, Hattie. I just want you to be happy." I tried to smile and she came over to hug me. It struck me that she smelled different, like cloves and black licorice and cigarette smoke. Not like normal Hattie.

"Thanks, Vi," she said before settling back into the couch.

There was a brief pause in the room before Reina piped up excitedly, "So, how was it??"

"Amazing," Hattie gushed. "He's *so* sensual."

"Did you cum?" asked Sage. Hattie giggled and nodded.

"How many times?" asked Bianca.

"Three!"

"Not bad," said Reina.

"In a whole afternoon? I could do better," Sage teased with a wink. Despite my better judgement, my mind quickly flashed to her lips on mine and a small swell of pressure pulsed in my stomach.

"I'm sure you could, Casanova," said Reina. "But moving onto more important things — what's for dinner?" Even with all this talk of sex and romance, food was always top of mind for this coven.

OVER A HEAPING PLATE of fresh ravioli with freshly grated parmesan, Hattie looked around the coven. I could tell she was nervous. "So next week I can't make coven dinner," Hattie said, eyes now downcast.

"What do you mean?" asked Bianca.

"You've never missed a coven dinner," said Reina, brow furrowed.

"I promised Cas I'd be his date to some art opening," Hattie said quietly.

"Seriously?" asked Reina.

"He can't go alone?" I asked.

"I don't know . . . He said it was really important and he needed my support." Hattie's cheeks flushed red as she took in our astonished expressions. We always put each other and the coven first. None of us have ever put a man or relationship before the group. It's just not how we do things. We sat in awkward silence for what felt like ages.

Sage was the first to break. "I guess that's okay . . . right?" She looked around to each of us, unsure if that was the right answer. I didn't know what to say.

"Yeah, I mean, it sounds like you already made your mind up about it," said Bianca. Reina stayed quiet. I could feel her annoyance radiating from her dark curly hair like a halo.

"Sorry . . . it'll just be a one-time thing." Hattie shifted uncomfortably in her seat. She looked at me, wide eyed. I shrugged and gave her a small smile. Hattie deserved to find love, and I wanted her to be happy. But I never thought it would come at the expense of the coven. Then again, one night wasn't going to diminish what we had, right?

After dinner, Reina and Bianca wanted to head to The Tilted Hollow for drinks. Hattie was in no position to deny them, so she decided to tag along. "I'll get the first round," she offered, slinging her arm around Reina.

"Good, that's what I like to hear," Reina said with a smirk.

"Sure you all don't want to join?" asked Bianca, halfway through the door.

"I need a break from the boozing," I said.

"I'll make sure she stays sober," Sage smiled at me.

"Alrighty, then. See you later." After she closed the door, we could hear the echoes of the three of them talking animatedly as they descended the stairs.

"You okay?" Sage asked, turning to face me.

"Wanna go get ice cream?"

Sage smiled. "Sure."

"Good." I went to get my coat, hearing Sage chuckle behind me. "What?"

"Nothing, just still figuring you out, I guess," she mused.

"I don't like feelings. I don't like talking about them. I don't like having them. I'd much rather eat them," I said with a little smile.

"Better get you that ice cream stat, then."

"Exactly."

WE SAT across from each other in the small ice cream shop. Sage swirled her spoon through her scoop of strawberry ice cream while I took slow and deliberate bites of my salted caramel. The perfect combination of savory and sweet.

"You know, the Brooklyn Heights coven has been coming into the shop a lot," Sage said, as if she'd been mulling it over.

"Really? Seems a bit out of the way for them."

"I know, right? You'd think they'd go to that store in Cobble Hill since it's so much closer."

"How often are they coming in?" I asked.

"Like every other day. It rotates. Sometimes, it's Casimir. Other times, it's Nikki or Adeline. Yesterday Nikki and Adeline came in together . . . is that weird? Or am I just reading into it?"

"I mean, it's a little strange, I guess. Especially since it's not like the shop is anywhere near where they live."

"And they get a lot of stuff, too," Sage said. She had a strange expression on her face, like she was trying hard not to worry. "Like I'm having to reorder stock much more frequently— which is great for business— but it strikes me as off. Why do they need so many specialty herbs and candles and a lot of dead bees . . . like way more than any coven should ever need."

"Dead bees?" Sage nodded as she put a spoonful of ice cream to her lips. "I've never even used those in my practice."

"Yeah, it's not a commonly used item, at least not in Bushwick," Sage said. She was the expert, North Brooklyn's premiere purveyor of magical items.

"Do you know what they could be using it *for*?"

"Dead bees are sometimes used for chaos magic or hexes . . . sometimes witches use them as an adornment for their altars but they seem to need way too many for that to be the case. Something is definitely off about that group."

"I knew it!" I said defiantly, piercing my ice cream

with my spoon for emphasis. "Do you think Hattie has any idea?"

"I don't know," Sage shrugged. "Probably not, she seems pretty smitten."

I nodded, feeling nervous. "I just don't want her to get hurt," I said, looking down at my slowly melting scoop of ice cream.

"I know, me either. But all relationships go one of two ways. Either you're together forever or at some point you break up," Sage said. I could tell she was trying hard to be nonchalant. She brought another bite of strawberry ice cream to her mouth. Her lips were only a shade or two darker than the frozen dessert. "You know, I'm more concerned about Cas's coven in general than him dating Hattie," she added, swallowing.

"Do you really think something could be going on . . . something more nefarious?"

"Nefarious? I don't know about that . . . but I just have a weird feeling about him, about *them*."

"Yeah, they were weird. And not in a fun way," I added. Sage smirked as she scraped her spoon across the bottom of her cup, trying to eke out one last taste.

I finished my ice cream and we headed back out into the Brooklyn night, winding our way through neighborhood streets. Neither of us were ready to call it a night. I didn't want to go home to an empty apartment, and Jackson was working the evening shift at Three of Cups.

Sage and I found ourselves ambling along the footpath in McCarren Park. We decided to sit down on a cold bench and watch a group of people playing baseball. It was chilly out, so we were basically alone. I leaned into Sage, without thinking, as the early spring chill stung my bare face.

Her shearling collar felt nubby against my skin as I rested my head on her shoulder. The familiar scent of lavender and vetiver filled my nose as she leaned into me, placing her head atop my own. We sat, silent, watching the people play ball in the lit-up baseball diamond. A gust of wind flew through the open field, kicking up a tiny amount of dirt with it. It swirled in the air, hovering above the ground before settling back down.

"Did you play any sports when you were little?" asked Sage.

"I played soccer as a young kid and some volley-ball in middle school," I said.

"I'd love to see you in those little shorts now," mused Sage with an impish chuckle.

"I bet you would . . ." *Stop flirting, Violet. Why was that so difficult?* "What about you? I feel like you were a swimmer or diver— something aquatic."

"Bingo. I swam in high school. What gave it away?"

"Just a feeling. And those long arms. Had to put them to good use," I joked.

"I miss swimming," she said. "Not the competi-tive aspect, but the meditative part, lap after lap. Just me and the water; it was very zen."

"Sounds nice."

"Maybe one day we can all go swimming sometime." I immediately thought of her lithe body gliding through the water like a mermaid.

"That would be fun. A little coven field trip." I sighed into the night, as we huddled together on the bench for warmth. Sexual tension be damned. We were really good friends, and this was a good friend hang out.

CHAPTER NINE

The sky was bucketing rain down on Brooklyn as Sage and I huddled under her clear umbrella. Raindrops streaked across the plastic like wet polka dots. We were headed to grab a drink at Three of Cups, since Mariah and Jackson were both working that night.

As we passed by the plant shop where Hattie worked, Sage suggested we pop inside to dry off. She gave the umbrella a quick shake before leading me by the hand inside.

Hattie stood over a table of ferns, misting them ever so gently. "Oh, hi," she said, looking up with a smile.

"Hello, my darling fern whisperer," I said.

"Maidenhairs can be very finicky, I'll have you know," she said teasingly.

"I'm sure," said Sage with a wink.

"What are you all up to?" Hattie asked, adjusting a fern leaf with care.

"We were going to grab a drink at Three of Cups, but figured we'd take a break from the rain and see you," said Sage.

"Yeah, what time are you off? Wanna join?" I added.

"I'm off at 5:30, so in a few minutes. Just needed to wrap up the ferns."

"Perfect," I said.

Hattie finished misting the precious ferns, silently mouthing a growth charm under her breath, and disappeared into the back of the shop. She returned with her bag. But her face had slackened as if half asleep.

"You okay?" Sage asked.

Hattie nodded, but her eyes stared blankly past us. I turned around to see what she was looking at, but nothing of note was there. The vibe had changed fast, and I was confused.

"Alright, then let's go grab a drink then?" I said, trying to pull Hattie back into the present with us.

"I'm so sorry, but I won't be able to join," Hattie said flatly. "I have some business I must attend to, but I'll see you later." She gave us each a curt nod, her eyes still unfocused. Then she walked out the shop door, leaving Sage and I standing by the ferns still.

"What was that?" Sage asked, turning to me.

"I have no idea . . . that wasn't our Hattie though."

"No," she paused, chewing on her bottom lip. "I think we should follow her."

"God, should we?"

"Yeah, something isn't right."

"Well, I can't argue with that," I said. "But following her seems . . . a little extreme, no?"

"I don't think so. Aren't you worried about her?! She's been acting kind of erratic since she started dating Cas."

"You're right. It's weird." I sighed. "Let's follow her like a couple of creeps and make sure she's okay"

Outside, Sage spread open the damp umbrella and began leading us down the sidewalk. She was sure to stay enough paces behind Hattie to go unnoticed. But Hattie never looked back.

We followed her down into the Bedford Avenue subway station and onto the L train, steps slick from the rain. She walked off the platform straight onto the subway car as if gliding on a track. Sage and I glanced at each other as we took a seat. Hattie still hadn't noticed us, and a wave of nervousness flitted through my body.

Hattie sat at the other end of the subway car, staring straight ahead. Not looking at a thing. Her eyes were glassy and her face totally vacant. When the train pulled into Canal Street, Hattie stood and waited for the doors to open. Sage and I followed, getting out at our end of the car as soon as the door opened.

We kept following Hattie, making sure to stay a number of paces behind her as we bobbed and weaved through the throngs of people wielding big black umbrellas. Hattie seemed laser focused, her head staying rigid as she kept her umbrella perfectly still even against the jostle of the street. Her body didn't have the casual swing that she typically carried. Sage looked at me, brow furrowed in concern.

Hattie climbed the steps, departing the station. By this point, it was clear we weren't at risk of her turning around to catch us. It was as if Hattie was a chess piece being played by an unseen force. She walked steadily and without any hesitation, each footstep planned. We followed her through China-town, doing our best not to be distracted by the cascade of delicious smells— roast duck, scallions, hot frying oil, and the rich burn of incense. My stomach grumbled as we passed by the parade of restaurants.

Hattie turned down Pell and then Doyers, the tiny narrow alleyway of a street once notorious for murders and now visited by hungry rain-soaked tourists. She buzzed a dented metal door next to a noodle shop and slipped behind the door without a sound. Sage sprinted forward to catch the door with her slender hand, before we could get locked out.

She turned to me and whispered, "Should we go inside?"

I nodded, and we entered the dimly lit stairwell. Hattie's boots rhythmically clacked on each step, reverberating through the chamber as we began to climb the stairs one flight behind her.

We heard her knock on a door from what sounded like the top floor, followed by a creaking door opening and a voice saying, "Come in, come in." The door closed. I felt a shiver down my spine. Sage and I exchanged looks as we continued up the stairs. There was only one door at the top of the landing. We stood outside of it, unsure of what to do next.

"What now?" I watched Sage as she leaned her ear to the door. "Can you hear anything?"

"Only a little bit, nothing too clear," she whispered. She slipped her canvas tote bag off her shoulder and began to dig around, eventually finding an amber glass bottle. "Ginkgo biloba and spearmint tincture," she explained. Ironically, Hattie had been the crafter of the tincture, what with her being the most powerful herbalist and alchemist we knew. She opened her mouth and dropped the elixir onto her tongue before handing it to me. I did the same, closing my eyes. I took three slow, deep breaths as I concentrated hard on what I could hear. Sounds quickly became sharper and more amplified.

I pressed my ear to the cold door beside Sage. "And when you're ready, you'll approach the altar," said a voice that sounded like liquid velvet. *Nikki.* It had to be Nikki. I was certain Adeline and Casimir were on the other side of the door as well. "Remember, today we are only working with the element of earth."

"That means skin, faces, cellulite, wrinkles . . . your Upper East Side derms can't tackle it the way we can, ladies," Adeline's voice punctured the room like a needle. A few small knowing laughs called out.

The front door's buzzer rang out from the other

side of the door, and I heard the rustle of quick steps coming towards the door. Sage and I froze, eyes on each other. A button on the other side clicked as the heavy metal door downstairs opened. We stood, silently making our way back down the stairs. I kept my head down, hoping I'd be able to sneak a glance at whoever was coming without them spotting me. A woman came in a frenzy up the stairs, a large leather Louis Vuitton checkered-printed tote bag swinging from her shoulders and her blonde hair damp from the rain. She didn't even acknowledge us as she passed. Thank god.

When Sage and I got outside the building, we both let out a loud exhale. Anxiety and adrenaline were coursing through my veins. I began to shake my wrists and hands, trying to release the tension I'd been holding the last twenty or so minutes. "What do you think that was?" I asked.

"Something shady, that's all I know," said Sage as she ran her fingers through her short crop of turquoise hair. The rain had softened to a drizzle now.

"Were they doing black market Botox? *Faces, wrinkles . . .*"

"Maybe. Probably not botulism though. I have a feeling there's a reason they've co-opted Hattie."

"She does make a mean body scrub," I joked, though it didn't feel very funny.

"Did the academy teach you girls about glamours?" Sage wasn't laughing. Her green eyes narrowed as I shook my head no.

"Not really. I mean, we learned about their history I guess, but we weren't taught them. It's against ethics."

"Violet, you can't be that naive."

"What?"

"Just because *you* may live by a code of ethics, does not mean every witch does. Not everyone goes to an academy, and even if they do, it doesn't mean they care about morality or following 'the rules.'" She made air-quotations for emphasis as I watched her talk. I felt defensive. I never would have called myself naive, but maybe I was. Maybe naivete was just half a step away from being privileged. And privileged I certainly was, that I couldn't argue with.

"With the right amount of skills and enough power, a witch can do *almost* anything modern plastic surgery can."

"What, like nose jobs?" I asked sarcastically.

"Yes, actually. And Hattie is powerful and skilled enough with herbs that she could probably. Not like a surgical nose job, but craft the right serums and elixirs and salves . . . I wouldn't be surprised if she'd be able to change the appearance of someone's nose. At least for a little while . . ."

My jaw literally dropped. I stood there, dumb-struck, with my mouth agape. That kind of magic was not something I had ever learned about. It sounded ridiculous.

"Don't look so shocked, Vi."

"Hattie would never-"

"That wasn't Hattie the way we know Hattie,

though," Sage said. Her voice was sharp. I nodded slowly. Hattie had clearly been steered there— her movements and the glassy eyes. I don't know who had compelled her to do this, but I'd guess Casimir was their hitman for Hattie.

"Shit," I sighed. Sage put her arm around me and gave it a squeeze.

"Yep . . ." she nodded.

"This is bad. We're going to have to tell Bianca and Reina," I said. My heart was sinking. How were we going to get Hattie out of this?

"Yeah . . . I can't believe those fuckers would actually put her under a compulsion like that." Her nostrils flared, angry.

My head felt hot as my ears began to ring. I was so angry; I wish I could hex all three of those witches. Why did I have to have ethics!? I let out a loud, frustrated groan into the night.

"Same . . . would dumplings help, Violet?"

"I think they're the only thing that can help right now." If I couldn't do anything to save Hattie right now, I'd eat my weight in dumplings until my rage felt under control.

CHAPTER TEN

The next day Sage had invited the coven, minus Hattie, to Light and Shadow after hours. After last night, we had to figure out what was going on. And we *needed* to work together to get Hattie out of this mess and safe from this trio of shady—or should I say low-key evil— witches.

"Where's Hattie?" asked Reina as she came into the store, the bell on the door tinkling behind her.

"She's not coming . . . because we need to talk about her and this new relationship with Cas," said Sage. Bianca arched her eyebrow as Reina leaned against a crystal-covered table.

"We're concerned about it," I began. "Sage and I ran into her the other night and something was wrong. To be honest, it was really scary."

"What are you talking about?" asked Bianca.

"Well, we ended up following her to Chinatown. It seemed like she was under a compulsion— eyes glassy and movements almost robotic. She ended up at some kind of meeting being led by Nikki, Adeline, and Casimir." Sage stopped, taking in Reina's and Bianca's reactions. They looked skeptical, exactly how I had felt before last night.

"It's true, and I know it sounds far-fetched . . . but it sounds like they're running some kind of occult augmentation scheme," I explained. They had to understand how upsetting it had been—seeing Hattie like that. "She was like a zombie, like a shell of herself. It was really freaky."

Bianca began to laugh. "Seriously? That's ridiculous," she said. Reina shifted her weight and pursed her lips. "Do you believe this, Rei?"

"I think . . . I think something is really wrong with Hattie. And something is wrong with those three Brooklyn Heights witches," she sighed.

"But compulsion? Occult plastic surgery? That's wild," insisted Bianca. "Don't you think we would have at least heard about something like that going on? At least rumors . . ." She was right, so much of the underground community was built on sharing and exchanging magic and ideas. It's how spells and charms were able to evolve and mutate. Magic wasn't a stagnant thing; it was ever-changing.

"Yeah, of course, it's wild, but who's to say that it's not what is happening," said Reina, her brow furrowed. "I mean, just think of that house and those clothes, their whole lifestyle is excessive and expensive. How do you think they can afford all of that?"

"I don't know," Bianca shrugged, looking slightly resigned. "But why would Hattie be involved?"

"Why do you *think*? Who do we all turn to for the most potent and efficient tinctures and tonics?" demanded Sage. "I refer my best customers to her when they need something complicated or specialized."

"She does have a gift," Bianca agreed quietly.

"So, what exactly happened when you followed her? Walk us through it," said Reina. Sage launched into a detailed retelling of everything we saw and heard that night. Bianca and Reina listened, rapt, their faces almost dumbfounded.

"You know . . . there have been a few nights where Hattie's seemed a little distant," said Reina as Sage finished.

"Really?" I asked.

Reina nodded. She looked worried. "Yeah, almost like she's taken Xanax or something. A little too calm for Hattie, a little too checked out. Not our usual bubbly, fussing-over-everything Hattie . . . I've never really seen her like that."

"Damn," murmured Bianca. "So, what do we do then? How do we even handle magic like this?" We all stood quietly, searching for our own answers, worried about our Hattie.

Finally, Sage spoke. "I know Violet doesn't have any experience with them, but do either of you ever play around with glamours?" She looked at Reina and Bianca. Reina shook her head no. But to my surprise, Bianca slowly nodded yes.

"Only a little," she said, looking guilty.

"Really?" I asked. As soon as I said it, I realized I sounded a little too judgmental.

"It's nothing to be ashamed of," said Sage. "It's totally fine to practice and play around with your craft however you see fit, as long as you aren't harming anyone or yourself. At least, that's how *I* feel." Sage shot me a glance.

Bianca's face relaxed. "Thanks," she said with a slight smile.

"What have you tried?" asked Reina.

"Mostly stuff with my hair, seeing if I could make it platinum without the bleach. It didn't last long enough though, and I couldn't figure out how to extend it," she said.

"I can give you some books to help with that," said Sage.

"Wait— is your hair—" I began. Sage nodded, running her hands through her short turquoise hair. "It's really a glamour?"

"Yep," she said. Damn, so that was why it always looked so freaking good.

"That's so fucking cool," said Bianca.

Sage laughed, trying to play it humble. "To think of all the things that academy of yours didn't teach you girls . . ." She smirked.

"Seriously," agreed Reina.

"Okay, so what do glamours have to do with this plan of yours?" I asked Sage.

"I think we need to go undercover, or at least one of us does. We can pool our magic to make it easier, do a glamour on one of us and then pretend to be, like, an Upper East Side mom in search of their services."

Well, that sounds only mildly terrifying.

"Let's do it," said Reina. She took a deep breath. "We need to get Hattie out of this mess."

"I'm game," agreed Bianca.

"Me too," I said, thinking of Hattie's big blue eyes glazed over. It made me angry, frightened even, just thinking about how someone could do a compulsion like that on an innocent person. And Hattie of all people, who would never hurt a fly and believed the best in people. All she wanted was to find love, and this is what she gets? *Oh hell no.* "I'll do it, I'll go undercover" I added, before I could second guess myself. Before I could let myself admit I was afraid.

"You will?" asked Sage, surprised. She searched my face, looking like she had more to say. I nodded and Sage kept her mouth shut.

"What if something goes wrong? Or they figure it out?" asked Bianca. "I don't want Violet getting hurt."

"Yeah . . ." said Reina, her brow furrowed in thought. "Vi, do you think Jackson could help us? Maybe like be your bodyguard or something? Stand outside and make sure you're safe?"

"Yes! And he has those crazy wolf ears, he'd be able to hear what's going on and make sure you're okay the whole time," said Bianca.

"Do we really want to get someone outside of the coven involved?" asked Sage. She looked concerned, not a fan of this idea.

"I mean, he *is* her mate. It's not like he doesn't know we're all witches," said Bianca. "Vi, do you think he'd be game?"

"I'll talk to him about it." But I already knew Jackson would do anything to keep me from harm.

"He will definitely want to help. Besides, he'd be worried about you otherwise. You know how protective he gets," she continued.

"Yeah, I'm sure he will." And I knew, of course, she was right.

"Great, that would be helpful," conceded Sage.

"So where are these books on glamours?" asked Bianca excitedly, her fear for Hattie momentarily displaced at the thought of new magic.

Sage walked over to the bookshelves and ran a long slender finger along their spines. She pulled out a select few, each with alluring jewel-toned covers, and stacked them in the crook of her arm. "You girls should all give these a read," she said, plopping the pile of books down on the store counter. "And we can start doing some practice sessions together."

We each took a few from the hefty stack, slipping the books into our bags. "Is everyone free tomorrow night?" asked Reina. "We can't put this off. I'm worried Hattie is in real danger."

"I can make it work," I said. Sage and Bianca nodded in agreement, eager to take action.

"We need to get home, then, and start studying," said Bianca.

We all hugged goodbye. Even with the excited anticipation of learning glamours, there was a solemn atmosphere, like the air was weighted. Nothing like our usual coven vibes. We waited outside as Sage pulled down the gate and locked up the Light and Shadow storefront.

"Get home safely," I said.

"See you all tomorrow," Sage replied with a wave as she turned on her heel heading towards her place.

I FELL ASLEEP the night before reading about glamours, devouring each page as fast as I could. This kind of magic had been kept from us at the academy. Now that I had a taste, I couldn't get enough. I needed to know everything I could about glamours. The next morning, I awoke groggily, my face stuck to the book. I peeled myself off my bed and wandered into the kitchen to make coffee. The apartment was quiet, Bianca's door shut.

As I turned on the coffee pot, I heard Bianca emerge from her room. She walked into the kitchen; her bleached mane piled messily atop her head.

"Morning," I said.

"Morning," Bianca said with a yawn. "I took the day off so I could finish reading before tonight." She folded herself into a kitchen chair and wrapped her arms around herself. "I can't believe this is happening."

"I know . . . well, at least we can lay on the couch all day and study, like old times," I said, trying to lighten the mood.

"Yeah," she sighed wistfully. "Such simpler times."

"Truly . . ." I said as I grabbed the half and half from the fridge. "I am worried about Hattie, though."

"Me too. But she will be okay. we will make sure of it . . ." I watched Bianca, but I wasn't sure I believed her. "It's pretty crazy, though. All this Trio stuff and the glamours. Aren't you pissed that the academy didn't teach us that kind of stuff?"

I poured the hot coffee into my mug, considering the question. I watched the dark liquid swirl into the half and half. "I guess."

"Well, *I* am. It's like we were robbed of a full education."

"But, isn't magic like that . . . *unethical*?"

"Unethical? It depends on how you use it, Violet. And that shouldn't preclude the academy from teaching us glamour magic. People can make fucked up things like bombs from science and math— should they stop teaching that in schools?" She undid her messy bun and ran her fingers through her tangled bleached hair, sighing frustratedly. I don't know why the academy didn't teach us certain kinds of magic. But right now all I could think about was getting Hattie away from the Trio. I needed to stay focused and not let my anger or resentment get the best of me.

"Yeah, that's a good point." I sat down across from her and sipped my coffee. "Makes me wonder what else they didn't teach us . . ." All those spells and rituals we weren't taught that I'd only ever heard whisperings or rumors about. Now I had to wonder what all was out there? What magic was out there that I had never even heard of or learned about?

"Exactly!" Bianca cried out, gesticulating wildly with her hands. "It's fucked up."

"I know. Like how much knowledge and power has been kept from us? And why?"

"Yep," Bianca nodded emphatically. Then she looked at me, as if she'd just thought of something. "Are you still taking Jackson home this weekend to meet your mom?"

"Yeah. I'm nervous . . ."

"*Aw* honey. Don't be. But maybe you can ask your mom about glamours . . . like was everyone hiding this kind of magic from us? Or are we going to blow their minds with this information?! Why did they even send us to the academy? Apparently, we could have learned more on our own as hedge witches," she ranted exasperatedly.

"I'll ask, but B, don't let this work you up so much," I sighed.

"Well, I think we should all be angrier," she snapped.

CHAPTER ELEVEN

Jackson sat behind the wheel, fingers tight on the faux leather, as he drove us through the winding, wooded backroads of upstate. We were only a couple hours outside the city, but it already felt like another planet. The air was crisp and clean, and in every direction you could see budding greenery. Spindly trees just beginning to bloom with new growth cast long shadows across the road in the late afternoon sunlight. I watched branches strobe past the car as I told Jackson all about what Sage and I had discovered about the Trio and Hattie.

"And you really think they're running some kind of black-market magic scheme?"

"Yeah. And I *know* that sounds bizarre— occult plastic surgery. Bravo can't even make this shit up . . . if only Andy Cohen knew," I said, trying hard to make light of the situation. But it didn't quell the fear I still felt tight in my stomach.

"But Hattie is really in danger, you think?"

"I mean, it's not a good situation," I said. I tapped my fingers nervously against the car window. "There's no way of knowing really *how* dangerous it is, but being under compulsion is scary and wrong."

"Absolutely," he said, his brow furrowed in concern. "How can I help?"

"Well, here's the thing," I sighed. "I kinda need . . . a bodyguard."

"A bodyguard?" He glanced over at me, brows arched in confusion.

"I'm going undercover— I know that sounds wild, but this is our plan . . ." And I told him all about glamour magic and our decision to send me undercover to the next meeting the Trio was hosting that we knew about.

He stared at me in disbelief. "And you sure this is a good idea?"

"I mean, it's the best idea we could think of."

He sighed, chewing his bottom lip. "I just want you to be safe."

"I know."

"Of course, I'll help in any way I can, Vi." He rested one hand on my thigh and gave it a squeeze.

"So you'll do it then?"

"Yeah. If you're in, I'm in," he said resolutely.

His long fingers curled over my knee as I let out a sigh. "Good."

My muscles relaxed now that we had sorted that out. I watched the woods roll by as Jackson turned on the stereo. Smashing Pumpkins reverberated throughout the car as the familiar opening chords of "Cherub Rock" rang out.

"IT'S THE NEXT RIGHT," I said as I tapped the car window. Jackson flipped on the turn signal, rhythmic dings ringing out and clashing with the beat of the music that played on the car stereo.

"Is your mom's boyfriend going to be there?" asked Jackson, one hand on my thigh while the other gripped the steering wheel.

"Gideon? I don't think so, but you never know with Mom," I said.

He glanced over at me and smiled reassuringly. "It's going to be fine, Vi. I've got this."

"I'm not worried about *you*, Jack. She will adore you; I have no doubt. I just . . . we don't really have this kind of relationship, you know. She's never met anyone I've dated."

"Well, to be fair, you haven't ever really dated anyone," he teased.

I let out a faux scoff before giggling. "Fair, but I liked it that way."

"I know you did," he sighed. "And then I came around and messed it all up for you."

"Yeah, you're a real force of destruction," I laughed.

Jackson hummed along to the radio as we rounded the corner, turning onto my old street. I took a few deep breaths and tried to calm my lingering nerves. Was this normal? I'd never had a boyfriend before; I'd never been in love before Jackson. And now my past and present were about to collide. It all felt so new and unknown. And I hated the unknown. To add to my baseline jitters of my first ever boyfriend meeting my mom, the fact that said boyfriend was a lycanthrope— a legit werewolf— well, that just nearly pushed my nerves over the edge.

"Vi, it's going to be okay," Jackson said, sounding calm. I exhaled slowly. "That's good, babe. Deep breaths." I nodded, breathing in and out slowly, rhythmically as I watched old familiar houses roll by.

When my parents split, my mom got the house where I grew up. My dad didn't even bother to fight her on it. He let her have it, and he moved to the city. Even though he was only on the Upper West Side, I didn't see him often. He had a new wife, Sherry. She was a beautiful woman ten years his junior. Just the kind of girl to get magic Botox. My dad spent a lot of time with her eleven-year-old son, JJ. I'd only met the kid a handful of times over the years. He liked video games and baseball. That's about the extent of what I knew about him. I didn't care to learn more. My dad seemed really happy in this new iteration of his life, and I felt it best to let him enjoy it. Without me.

Don't get me wrong, I loved my dad. I'd say our relationship was even pleasant most of the time, but I didn't like being reminded of the past. *My* past. If I spent too much time around my dad, I'd begin to feel those old wounds open. I'd start to have flashbacks of my parents' fights, the nights he'd storm out and head to his office to drink and crash there instead. My parents' relationship had grown toxic the longer they were together. It took them seventeen years to call it quits, three more to heal and act civilly around the other. Now they were amicable enough if they ever had to interact. I made sure that wasn't much, since I was grown up now and living on my own.

I looked out the window as the car wove through the tall trees. The sky was a bright cerulean blue. It was a cold day in the middle of March, the last vestiges of winter remained in the chilly air. If I looked carefully, I could see the beginnings of green leaves poking their little heads out from the branches.

"Okay, so it's the second house on the left this next block." I pointed down the street, directing Jackson.

"You ready?" he asked softly.

I let out a long sigh, and he laughed. "Yeah, as ready as I'll ever be."

I had a fine relationship with my mom. Good even compared to my dad. It wasn't contentious, per se, it just wasn't like the fuzzy mother-daughter relationships I saw on television. Nobody would ever mistake us for the Gilmore Girls.

My mom was always fun to be around, though. She was smart, funny, and gregarious. But she was also painfully independent and could be selfish at times. Maeve did what she wanted when she wanted to, that's always how it had been. She was there for me growing up, but it could sometimes feel like I was a side character in my own life in those early teen years, when my parents' fighting was at its worst. I was pulled into their drama, instead of being allowed to have drama of my own like a normal teenage girl

Jackson pulled the car into the driveway of our old Victorian house that my mom had painted lavender after my dad left. My mom swung open the front door and began waving enthusiastically from the veranda.

"Here we go," I said, almost to myself, as I opened the door.

"Baby!! You're here!" my mom called out as she rushed towards us, arms open wide. She wrapped me in her long, thin arms and held me tightly. "It's so good to see you," she murmured into my hair. I squeezed her back warmly as the familiar smell of gardenia flooded my nostrils.

"It's good to see you too, mom," I said. And I meant it. My mom had her faults, but, above anything, she always made me feel loved.

I stepped away and grabbed Jackson's hand, pulling him towards us. "Mom, this is Jackson."

"Hi, Mrs. Byrne, thank you for having me," Jackson said, trying hard to be polite.

"Please! Call me Maeve. You are welcome here anytime," my mom said as she gave Jackson a hug. "It is so nice to meet you!"

"Likewise," he said as he went to the trunk of the rental car, pulling out our overnight bags.

My mom led us both inside as her dog Zadie ran into the foyer. Zadie was a small mutt with curly white hair. My mom had adopted her during my junior year at the academy, after our beloved cat Linus passed away. Zadie snapped happily at our heels, excited to have me home.

I leaned down to scratch Zadie as she placed her tiny paws on my knees and began to lick my nose. "Hi, sweet girl," I cooed.

Jackson crouched down beside me and greeted Zadie with total affection. She went wild, licking every inch of his face as her tail wagged frantically. I wondered if Zadie could tell Jackson was a lycanthrope, if she could smell it on him the way he could smell it on other wolves. He scooped her up in his arms and held the little dog to his chest as he scratched behind her ears. "I think she likes me," he said, smiling. I couldn't help but laugh as Zadie began to lick inside his ear.

"Zadie, let the man be," my mom said. "She's such a flirt."

"Ah, it's fine, I love dogs," Jackson laughed. His eyes flashed towards me as he gave me a knowing wink. He set Zadie down on the floor.

"So, can I get you anything to drink or eat? I stocked up," Mom said.

"Water would be great, mom, thanks," I said as we followed her into the kitchen.

Mom pulled two glasses out of the cupboard, filling them with water from a stylish vintage glass pitcher. The kitchen, as always, was full of flowers— almost every surface was adorned with some kind of vase and bundle of blooms. Mom loved gardening and adored flowers. I eyed the largest vase that held center stage on the breakfast table. It was bursting with an array of pink and coral roses, towering white snapdragons, and little clusters of delicate blue forget-me-nots.

"I didn't grow those . . . they're from Gideon," she said. Her face lit up every time she mentioned her boyfriend.

"Wow, he did good. Any special occasion?" I asked.

"Nope," she smiled. "Just because."

"I should take notes," Jackson said. Mom chuckled as she handed us our water. We sat around the breakfast table and admired the flowers as we rehydrated from the car ride. Recycled air always makes me parched.

Jackson pointed out a framed photo hung on the wall of me in a big blue tutu and bedazzled leotard. Mom pulled Zadie up into her lap, petting her as she told Jackson about my first dance recital.

"She was so cute, but she got stage fright and just froze as all the other little girls danced around her."

"In my defense, I was only four," I said.

"True, it's a lot to ask of a four year old. And slowly other little girls forgot the moves and started to join you just standing there like tiny deer caught in headlights. The parents all had to stifle a laugh. It was just so adorable," Maeve said with a nostalgic smile.

"I bet Vi was the cutest kid," Jackson mused.

"Oh, she was, with these black ringlets and big

hazel eyes . . . I'll have to pull out some photo albums— "

"Mom—"

"What? This is what moms do!"

"I'd love to see them, Mrs. Byrne," Jackson said. He was being so nice—typical Jackson, the perfect boyfriend. I don't know how I got so lucky.

"Please, it's Maeve!" my mom insisted.

After more tales from the past, Jackson excused himself to the restroom. When he was fully out of earshot— at least for a human, but mom didn't know about his lycanthropy— she leaned in to me.

"Sweetie, he *knows*, right? About you? About us?" she whispered.

"Yes, he knows," I reassured her. "He knows we're witches, and he knows about my coven."

"And he wasn't skeptical? Judgmental? Freaked out?"

"Nope."

"Okay, good, good . . ." She let out a sigh of relief. "And has he met the girls?"

"Yep, he's met them all— Bianca, Hattie, Reina, Sage— the whole coven. They really like him." I grabbed her hand and gave it a squeeze. Her face relaxed and she smiled.

"Good. . . Gideon will be joining us for dinner tonight, by the way. He's excited to see you and to meet Jackson."

"Okay, that's cool. Has he joined your coven?"

"No, no, no . . . that's too much for me to handle. He's been a part of his own coven for many years, anyway." After dealing with my father's resentment towards her powers, mom vowed to only ever date another witch.

A FEW HOURS LATER, the doorbell rang out, and I heard my mother greet Gideon at the door. Jackson and I were upstairs in my childhood bedroom freshening up after our long drive. The walls in my room were still painted a brilliant shade of lilac, not dissimilar to the outside of our old Victorian house. *Violet for violet,* my parents used to say. There were pictures of Bianca and my high school friends in frames on my dresser and old movie stubs tucked into the wooden frame of my mirror. It was like stepping into a time warp; it was hard not to feel sixteen again when I was home.

Jackson pulled a fresh heathered burgundy sweater over his head and bunched the sleeves up to his elbows. He caught me admiring his taut forearms. "Hey, now, don't get too excited before dinner," he said with a teasing smile.

"You better keep those arms covered then, mister," I joked.

I changed into a loose grey cowl-necked sweater dress and paired it with big fuzzy socks to keep my feet warm. No need for shoes or anything too fancy for dinner at home. Jackson squeezed my hip and leaned in to give me a kiss. "You're so cute," he murmured.

"Oh yeah?" I flirted as I gave him a final kiss before heading downstairs.

Gideon was in the kitchen, talking with my mother as she cooked. He uncorked a bottle of wine as he spotted me enter the room with Jackson. "And here are the guests of honor!" he called out.

"Hi Gideon, it's good to see you," I said, as I gave him a hug. "This is my boyfriend, Jackson."

Jackson reached out a hand and they shook, man to man. Or man to wolf. "Hi, nice to meet you," he said.

"Good handshake," commented Gideon. "Maeve told me she's already a fan of yours."

"It's true," my mom said as she stirred the large pot of vegetarian chili simmering atop the stove. "Go ahead and sit down in the dining room, I'm about to start plating the macaroni."

"Oh my god, I haven't had chili-mac in ages."

"It was always your favorite when you were little."

"Thanks, mom." I leaned in and kissed her on the cheek, touched that she had made it especially for me.

Gideon poured us each a glass of wine and handed them to us to carry into the dining room on the other side of the kitchen. Mom had lit candles and set out the bouquet from Gideon in the middle of the old oval cherrywood dining table.

Soon we were all seated and enjoying the chili-mac and fresh endive salad with my mom's special vinaigrette. She liked to enchant her vinaigrette with special herbs she'd grown in her garden. It was her secret to getting me to eat greens when I was a kid. It made the flavors extra light and fresh, so that you wanted to keep taking bite after bite.

I looked around the table, watching Jackson talk to my mom and Gideon. Everyone seemed to be enjoying themselves. I was surprised at how well it was all going. Was this what a normal functioning family looked like? People getting along and enjoying each other's company. Nobody verbally sparred over dinner rolls after too many beers. I bet this felt familiar to Jackson, whereas it felt foreign— but nice— to me.

"So how did you two meet?" Jackson asked between bites of chili-mac.

Gideon smiled and took my mother's hand lovingly. Before he could speak, my mom answered for him. "We met at a Beltane party a few years ago. Well, it really was more like a festival."

"There were covens and witches from all over New York gathering in this field a few miles from here, and we bumped into each other while waiting to use the toilets," Gideon laughed.

"I locked eyes with him, and I just knew we were going to fall in love," my mom said as she took a sip of wine.

"Maeve's hair was so messy and windswept and she had all these flowers pinned in it. She looked like a goddess that had somehow found herself on earth." Gideon looked at my mother, his eyes all lit up. I could see the love there on his face the way I could see it when Jackson looked at me. I was happy my mom had found a partner like Gideon. After all this time.

"That's so sweet," Jackson said.

"Yeah, it's a cute story, right?" Maeve said as she smiled at Gideon.

I chewed a bite of salad as I silently admired everyone's happy faces in the candlelight. Everybody was eating and sipping wine contentedly. It was all so peaceful and effortless.

"How are the girls, Vi?" Maeve asked, twirling her fork in her chili-mac.

"They're great. We've been really good . . . and Bianca started dating this demonologist."

"Ah yes, Giulia told me about him. B is smitten apparently," she said. I should have known. Bianca and her mom Giulia shared everything. They talked on the phone at least twice a day, and Bianca couldn't keep a secret from her mom even if she tried.

"Yeah, they seem to really like each other," I said.

"And what about that Sage? You two were getting to be really close, right?" My stomach constricted into a knot. I hadn't spent any time alone with Sage since the night we kissed. I couldn't open that Pandora's box if I wanted to protect my relationship with Jackson. Next to me, he shifted in his seat as he stared awkwardly at his plate.

"Um, she's good. Just busy with the shop I think," I said before taking a long drink of wine.

"Well, I can't wait to meet her next time I come

down to the city. She's the only one in your coven I don't know," mom said pointedly.

I wanted to get away from *this* topic of conversation as fast as I could. "Yeah, I'm sure you'll meet her soon," I said, trying to brush it off.

"Sage is great, Mrs. Byrne. You'll love her," Jackson said, smiling. The knot in my stomach tightened even more. Why did he have to be so nice?

"*Maeve*, Jackson, please call me Maeve. No need to be so formal," she said with a smile.

THAT NIGHT, after Gideon had left and Jackson, sleepy, ascended the stairs to go tuck himself into bed, my mom and I stayed up talking. She'd brewed a pot of home-grown chamomile that was charmed with a relaxation spell. We curled up on the couch in the old family room, just the two of us. I wrapped myself in one of the blankets my grandmother had knit decades ago. I liked feeling her close to me still, even though she was no longer in the earthly realm with us.

"You're really in love, aren't you?" Mom asked with a knowing smile.

"Yes." I couldn't help but sigh. Mom let out a soft laugh as I took a sip of my tea. The steam wafting up tickled my nose.

"I can see it all over your face, you're radiating a new energy. And god, Jackson is clearly head over heels . . . one look at him and it's obvious."

"Really?"

"Sweetie, when a man is in love, it's hard to ignore. He looks at you like he's a little puppy dog," she teased. Little did she know just how close to a puppy he was every full moon. "And you two seem really happy . . ." She trailed off, hinting at a *but* she didn't want to say.

"Go on . . ." I prompted.

"Is there something else going on?" She arched her eyebrows, as she sipped her tea—half concern, half motherly curiosity. I paused, debating whether I wanted to go there with my mom. We'd never talked about boys or relationships like this . . . I mean, I'd never really had anything to discuss. I'd always used dating as distractions, as amusing stories to be told later to the girls over wine. One-night stands and a handful of casual relationships lasting no longer than six weeks were just fodder for coven dinners. Not the sort of thing you talk about with your mom.

I knew I did *not* want to tell her about Jackson's secret, his lycanthropy. It wasn't my secret to divulge. And who knows what it would mean to her. I didn't want it to color how she viewed him. It might change nothing at all, but it wasn't a risk I wanted to take. Not all witches were so comfortable with lycanthropes. Some still held old beliefs that they were scary and unpredictable, prone to possessiveness and aggression. I didn't think my mom felt that way— we'd never talked about werewolves really—but I didn't feel like I needed to bring it up to her.

"No, Jackson and I are really happy," I insisted. "Just like you said."

"I can see *that*, honey. That wasn't really what I was referring to. I know there's something else on your mind."

"*Ugh* . . . Okay, there is," I sighed. "Why did you send me to the academy?"

"What do you mean? You wanted to go to Greenwood! It's one of the best academies in the country!"

"I know I did, but I didn't know there were other options."

"Sweetie, we looked at other schools, even regular colleges, but you always loved Greenwood best. Didn't you have a good time there?" She looked genuinely confused, even hurt that I would question our alma mater."I did, but mom, there was so much they didn't teach us. And that *you* didn't teach *me*. I've learned more from the underground scene in Brooklyn than I did in four years at the academy."

"Well, part of that is just growing up, Violet."

"That's not what I mean, mom. There's magic that they kept from us, that *you* kept from *me*."

Mom's face contorted, thinking hard. Then she signed, resigned, and began to nod. "That may be true . . . but it's more complicated than that."

"How so?" I snapped.

"Magic is nuanced and powerful and there are degrees of morality and intention and differing schools of thought . . ."

"No shit."

"*Violet*."

"*Mom*."

"You're acting like a child."

"Because you're treating me like a child! Of course, I understand that magic is *complicated*, but I feel like I wasn't prepared for life on my own as a witch."

"And what is it that you feel like was withheld?"

"So much! Glamour magic for one."

"Glamour magic? Violet, that's hardly life or death stuff."

"But isn't it my birthright as a witch to be taught and have access to *all* degrees of my power and capabilities?"

Mom paused, really thinking this over. "Perhaps," she said. "But is glamour magic really what you're upset about?"

"Not just glamour magic . . . I just feel like we should have been taught *everything*. Like what else about magic don't I know? I feel like an idiot. Like a sheltered little girl."

"You're not an idiot, Violet! My coven, all of whom went to Greenwood, does not practice glamour magic. And there are many witches who do not, because we don't believe it's morally right to alter appearances and other people's perspectives. Powerful glamour magic can manipulate the world around us and we don't have the right to play with others like that. We believe it is dishonest and deceitful. And we want to respect the natural world and how we were made."

"I get that," I let out a sigh, frustrated. "But shouldn't I be allowed to decide what's right for me — what *my* ethics and moral code is?"

"You do now. But I'm your mother, and raising a child means imparting my values on you and trying to set you up to be the best and happiest version of you. And with *your* children, you can make different choices."

I didn't have a clever retort for her. So, I pouted in silence as she watched. Slowly, I felt myself relent and my pout fade. As much as I hated to admit it, maybe my mom was right. She slid closer to me on the couch and wrapped an arm around me tenderly.

"Honey, I'm sorry you're upset. And I'm sorry you feel I withheld important knowledge from you. That was *never* my intention. I was just trying to raise you the best I knew how."

I let myself lean into her and flung my legs across her lap like I'd do when I was little. She held me and stroked my hair as we sat together quietly. After a few minutes, she asked softly. "Where did this all come from, Vi? Is it that hedge witch that joined your coven, Sage?"

I stiffened. "Huh?"

"Well, I know hedge witches tend to dabble in things other coven-ed or traditionally taught witches steer clear of . . . "

"Sage is a good person, mom."

"I'm sure she is. That's not what I'm saying at all, honey."

"Um. Okay . . ."

"I was just curious where all of this was coming from, that's all." I shrugged as I disentangled from her. I grabbed my mug of tea and folded my legs up crisscross under me.

"So there's nothing going on there?"

"Nope."

"Okay," mom said, looking unconvinced as she held her mug to her lips. "Nothing to do with that girl Sage?" *Shit.* No matter how hard you try, it's nearly impossible to keep a secret from your mom when she's a witch.

"What do you mean?" I did my best to keep my voice even keel. I didn't want to betray myself, especially to my mother.

"She's the newest witch in your life and you have all these questions now. And she owns that shop. I can only assume that she's introducing you to parts of the underground you and the other girls hadn't been exposed to before."

"Oh," I exhaled, relieved. "Yeah, she has. But don't worry, we're not like raising the dead or orchestrating bank heists with magic."

"But you've thought about it," she teased.

"Oh, loads," I joked.

"I love you, Violet. And I am so proud of you. I want you to know that." She looked at me so earnestly. Her hazel eyes, the same hue as mine, were wide and pleading. "I know we had some tricky years there when you were a teen, but I'm really glad you came to visit and brought Jackson. I want to be in your life more."

"Mom," I said softly. "I want that too. And I love you." I set my mug down and wrapped my arms around her. I buried my face in her hair and blinked back tears. I could tell from her shallow breathing she was crying. We held each other like that for what felt like forever. I sighed and closed my eyes, letting myself relax and, finally, be mothered.

CHAPTER TWELVE

I woke that morning curled into Jackson's back, as if to keep warm. I'd become used to sleeping with this large furnace now, and, on cold mornings, it came in handy. Beside me, he began to rustle awake and murmur groggily.

"Morning," I whispered into his back.

He rolled over to face me, eyes still closed. "Morning," he croaked. I smirked as I rubbed my head into his chest like a cat. We lay there, listening to my mother cook breakfast downstairs. The smell of bacon wafted upstairs, and Jackson began to stir. Typical wolf. Throw some meat in the frying pan and he was there.

He kissed the top of my head and got out of bed, grabbing his sweatshirt off the floor. "That smells delicious. I'm starving," he said as he pulled his sweatshirt on, his hair sticking out at funny angles.

"Babe, you might wanna comb your hair."

He shrugged and ran his fingers through his messy mane haphazardly. "Good enough," he said.

"You're so cute," I smiled up at him.

"You are, sleepyhead. Now, get up!" He picked up the sweater I'd draped over my wooden desk chair, tossing it at me. I tugged it on with a smile.

"Alright, let's go," I said, crawling out of bed. He wrapped his arms around me and kissed the top of my head, before we padded downstairs following the smell of bacon.

"There you kids are! Good morning!" My mom called over to us as we entered the kitchen. Strips of bacon bubbled atop the cast iron frying pan she was monitoring.

"Morning, Maeve. That smells incredible," Jackson said.

I hugged my mom from behind, as I watched the bacon sizzle and pop, little bursts of grease erupting in the air. "Morning, mommy," I said sleepily.

"Mommy? Wow, haven't heard that one in a while," she teased. I kissed her on the cheek and sat down at the breakfast table next to Jackson. Mom beamed at us as she turned the bacon. I felt a pang of guilt that I didn't come to see her more often.

"Can I help with anything?" Jackson asked.

"No, no, no! There's coffee ready in the pot, though. Help yourself," she said.

The three of us ate our eggs and bacon with thick pieces of rye toast from the local bakery—seriously delicious. We drank our coffee slowly as we sat around the table together. It was everything I'd wished for as a kid, an easy Sunday morning spent with family. No arguing, no passive aggressive comments, no awkward silences—just simple and peaceful.

After breakfast, Jackson and I cleaned up the kitchen for my mother before saying goodbye. We were headed to a nearby hiking trail on our way back to the city. I wanted to take him to a trail I used to walk with Bianca when I needed to be in nature and get out of my head. Or out of my house when my parents were fighting. Bianca and I would ride our bikes, peddling until our legs ached and we were out of breath. We'd dump our bikes behind old fallen branches and run into the woods until we felt miles away from the real world. It was the most liberating and cathartic feeling for my young self. Just me, Bianca, and the trees.

As we said goodbye on the porch of the old Victorian, I held my mom tight. "I love you," I murmured into her ear. The smell of gardenia mixed with her shampoo caused a bittersweet nostalgia to swell in my chest. I blinked back tears as I held onto her.

"I love you, too, Violet. And I'm so proud of the woman you've become. I know I don't tell you enough." My mom brushed my hair behind my ear as I blinked back tears. We had the same thick raven mane, though hers was now becoming streaked with silver.

"And, Jackson, it was so lovely to meet you. Please come back anytime." My mom hugged Jackson, his 6-foot frame towering over her petite 5-foot-

3. She was even tinier than I was at 5-foot-5, and always undeniably cute. That was the word all of my friends used to describe my mom— cute.

We drove away as she stood on the porch waving goodbye, as she held Zadie. Her smile was wide and genuine, and I realized that this trip had been something she and I had needed for a long time. I felt like I was finally letting go of all those years of fighting and resentment. My mom had done her best, and I really was lucky to have her. And I was excited for this new phase of our relationship. I was lighter and more open—a lot of that thanks to Jackson—and ready to let my mom in and accept her for who she was, not who I wanted her to be when I was younger.

THE SKY WAS BRIGHT BLUE, streaked with stratified clusters of white clouds. Winter's remaining dead leaves crunched underfoot as we walked along the trail's dirt path. I could finally feel spring coming in the air and took a deep, satisfied inhale.

"God, it's so good to get out of the city sometimes," I said.

Jackson nodded. "The air just hits differently up here, right?"

Out here in the country, smelling that fresh air, I wanted to run like a new foal finding its feet—like I did with Bianca when we were kids. After such a cold winter, a hint of spring was all I needed to feel ignited. I picked up the pace and even added a few playful skips. Jackson laughed, joining me until we were giddily skipping along like schoolchildren. I pumped my legs trying to keep up with him as tiny beads of sweat began to cling to my forehead. We slowed down, out of breath, as our laughter dissipated into the trees.

"So . . . what did you think of my mom?" I'd been dying to ask.

"I loved her. She's great. So fun and open. I didn't feel uncomfortable at all," he said.

"Yeah, it went a lot better than I expected."

"I know you were worried, but seriously, I had an amazing time, Violet." I nodded. After all my worrying, it really hadn't been such a big deal. I had been prepared for an awkward visit, full of laborious conversation and uncomfortable silences. Maybe even a fight. I had underestimated how *easy* my mom could be in social situations and how comfortable Jackson was in his own skin. It was one of the things I admired most about him.

We walked along the forest trail, listening to the birdsong coming from high up in the barren trees. Occasionally, Jackson would echo their tune with a whistle. But when I tried, I mostly spit with barely a note making it out, causing us to collapse into giggles.

After a long moment of admiring the wildlife, Jackson turned to me. "Come here," he said, taking my hand. He led me off the path. We wound through the naked trees, ducking under spindly branches beginning to sprout new leaves.

"Where are you taking me, Jack?" I asked coyly, purposefully playing dumb.

"Somewhere a little more private, where we can get better acquainted, my dear," Jackson said, playing along. "This little clearing here looks perfect." He twirled me around as if we were dancing. Then he pulled me into him.

I kissed him hard and wrapped my arms around his broad back, gripping him tightly. Our hands began to explore each other, hungry. Jackson slid his fingers in the waistband of my leggings and pulled them to my ankles, taking my underwear with them. I let out an excited gasp as he spun me around and kissed my neck. Arching my back, I pressed my ass into his crotch and could feel him stiff and ready. I reached behind me and fumbled with his pants until he sprung free.

"Oooooh," I cooed, as I ran my fingers over his body. He sighed softly and slid into me. I gripped a tree as he thrust into me rhythmically. With every motion, my moaning got louder. Thank god, the trail had seemed to be empty.

Jackson held onto my hip with one hand as he slid the other up under my sweatshirt and grasped my breast tightly. I groaned as warmth spread through my body like the roots of the trees that surrounded us. I held on tighter to the bark of the tree trunk as I pushed myself against him harder. He grunted and began to pant as we frantically moved our bodies together until we came.

We caught our breaths as I pulled back up my

underwear and leggings with a laugh. "Well, that was a nice surprise," I said.

Jackson chuckled and kissed me sweetly. "I just can't keep my hands off you, Violet," he teased.

"I know, and I like it."

We headed back to the trail and continued walking as the sun rose higher in the sky.

CHAPTER THIRTEEN

O n Monday night back in the city, Reina, Bianca, and I met Sage at Light and Shadow. The shop was closed for the evening, and Sage had set out an array of supplies for our practice session. Vials of honey and bundles of herbs, dried flowers, and feathers were laid atop a wooden table in the back room of the store.

"Okay, did everyone do their reading?" Sage asked, sounding like a strict schoolteacher. We all nodded. We were witches who always did their homework. "Good. We're going to need to work as efficiently as possible. I went ahead and printed this stock photo of a lady we can use as our guide for the glamour." Sage pulled out a sheet of paper that featured a woman who looked to be in her forties, with golden curls and tanned skin. A string of pearls hung around her neck. She looked like she played tennis in the Hamptons and went to important business dinners with her CEO husband.

"She's perfect," said Reina wryly.

"So that will be our map, right?" Bianca asked.

"Yep," Sage said, nodding. "Shall we get to it?"

"Yes," I said. Bianca and Reina nodded. There was a tense excitement in the air. As serious as the situation was with the Trio and Hattie, we couldn't help but look forward to practicing new magic.

And so, the ritual began. We moved about the space as if performing a choreographed, well-rehearsed dance in the way that only a close-knit coven could. Sage sprinkled salt across the table, drawing a large pentagram, as Reina placed a white pillar candle in each of its five points. Bianca lit them with closed eyes, swaying slightly as she funneled her magic into the ritual. I prayed over a large, glittering gold cluster of pyrite before placing it in the center of the pentagram. Sage poured the honey into a marbled soapstone mortar as Bianca sprinkled in crushed rose petals, thyme, and peppermint leaves. Reina took the pestle and began muddling the mixture together, muttering the incantation over it.

I placed a cluster of deep purple amethyst and a small pyramid of clear quartz next to the flickering candles as I held the vision of me transforming into the woman from the photograph in my mind's eye. We joined hands and hummed in unison, letting the vibrations fill the room like a swarm of bees.

"As above, so below. What has been will return again. In this world and those beyond," we chanted as Reina held up the mortar, tipping the syrupy elixir into my mouth. I swallowed, gulping it down, and

we repeated the chant a final time. The candles flickered wildly, casting frenetic shadows across the
shop's backroom as we crowded around an antique
gilded mirror leaning against the wall to watch our
magic unfold.

My wavy raven hair transformed into glossy
honey-blonde curls. I ran my fingers through my
new tresses in wonder. My nails were now longer
and shinier. My skin was bronzed like I'd just come
back from a tropical vacation— or a really good
spray-tan appointment. My nose was thinner and
more pointed, and my eyes were now a deep blue
instead of hazel. Delicate crow's feet punctuated
them, which helped me look older.

"Holy shit!" said Bianca.

"I can't believe that's really you, Vi," marveled
Reina.

My eyes were transfixed to my reflection. With
each new angle I turned my head, I tried to find the
traces of my old face. But the old familiar moles had
all been erased. The small scar next to my hairline
from falling off the swings when I was small had
disappeared. The smallest details had vanished. It
was both unnerving and thrilling—strange to see this
stranger's face looking back at me, but so exciting to
experience this new kind of magic.

"This is *freaky*," I said, glancing up to see Bianca
and Reina's mouths agape.

Sage started to laugh. "I have to admit, I'm pretty
impressed with us. I've never done a glamour this
complex."

"I really look like an Upper East Side mom," I said.

"Who has the nanny run to Pressed Juicery daily for her 3pm ginger and turmeric tonic," said Reina.

"While she's doing yoga downtown at Sky Ting and Instagramming it, naturally," added Bianca.

"Because she's soooo stressed out. Little Kinsley is never going to get into Dalton if that pre-k of hers keeps giving them snacks full of preservatives!" said Sage, as we all burst into laughter.

"We've created a monster . . . we shall name her Mindy," I said proudly.

"*Mindy*," they all cooed in unison, giggling.

"It's perfect," said Reina as she admired my new face. "Ladies, we did good. We should take a pic."

Bianca murmured in agreement as she pulled her phone out of her bag and began snapping rapid-fire photographs of me. We all crowded around her screen and looked at them in awe.

"Magic is wild," I said.

"I don't know if I'll ever be able to get over this," said Bianca. "It's crazy!"

"How long will I have to look like this?"

All the girls started to laugh, until Sage finally assuaged me. "At most, three hours . . . this isn't the strongest glamour. It's layered, sure, but it's not crafted for long term results like I imagine the Trio's are. That would be far more intense and draining for all of us."

"I'm seeing Jack later, though," I said.

"Ohhhh, don't worry. I have an antidote," Sage

said, as she rummaged in the cabinet and pulled out a small amber vial. "Here," she said, placing it in the palm of my hand. "It may take a little bit to work, though. Just put five drops on your tongue."

Watching myself in the mirror, I took five small drops straight on my tongue. My glamoured face slowly began to melt back into my familiar one. The nose plumped and shortened. My hair darkened, and my eyes returned to hazel like a mood ring changing colors. The tiny scar etched its way back onto my hairline last. And that's how I knew everything was back to normal. Slowly, the glamour undid itself, like watching a painter work in reverse.

"Incredible," whispered Bianca.

"How do you *feel*?" asked Reina.

"Fine, actually." I ran my hands over my arms, skimming all my familiar freckles and moles, making sure they were still there. It felt good to be back in my normal body. "I just wish I knew what to expect at the actual meeting." My stomach knotted nervously if I thought about that upcoming night for a moment too long. I had no idea what exactly happened behind that closed door. Of course, I wanted to find out, but I also wanted to make sure I would be safe—and that Hattie would be safe too.

"I know, same," said Reina. Bianca nodded in agreement.

"About that," Sage started. She held up a cluster of stones knitted together by silver swinging from a small leather loop like a pendulum. "I made this amulet for your protection." Sage pressed it into my palm as we all studied it. The talisman was made of three black stones— tourmaline, obsidian, and Apache tears from the look of it. I ran my thumb over their smooth tumbled faces.

"Thank you," I said as Sage watched me with worried eyes.

"Not that I think anything bad will happen to you . . . just figured we should be careful," Sage said, as I nodded solemnly. "Glamour magic isn't always pretty or easy."

"What are you alluding to?" Bianca said, her lips pursed in worry. My heartrate quickened as I scanned the girls' concerned faces.

"What am I missing?" I asked Sage.

"You know how they say beauty is pain?" I nodded. "Well . . . that can be true of intense, long lasting glamours. To create that kind of a transmutation and magical alteration . . . it might hurt."

"Why didn't you say this earlier?" snapped Bianca. My pulse was rising and had moved to my temples. It thumped loudly behind my eyes. "Are you okay, Vi?"

"Um . . ." was all I managed to stammer out. Reina grabbed my wrist, tightly wrapping her fingers around it. My pulse began to slow, and I took a deep breath.

"Good. Keep doing that," she said, trying to calm me down.

"Thanks, Rei." Reina's dark almond-shaped eyes crinkled reassuringly as she patted my hand.

"I promise you won't feel anything if you have the

amulet on you, Violet," said Sage. "I would never send you into a situation like that without protection."

"Okay," I said quietly. Though, this didn't assuage all my fears.

"I *promise*," she repeated. I nodded and looked at Bianca. She shifted in her black leather ankle booties, picking at the hem of her dress. She caught my gaze and stood up straight, giving me a little smile.

"It will all be fine, Vi. We've got your back," Bianca said.

"I know. And I want to do this for Hattie, no matter what. If they take a knife to my face, so be it . . ." They all looked blankly at me. "It's a joke, guys." Each of them let out an awkward chuckle. "There aren't going to be knives though, are there?" My stomach churned at that thought.

"No . . . well, I wouldn't think so. Haven't ever read anything about knives being involved in glamour magic," said Sage.

"If you want the knife, you have to go to an actual plastic surgeon, babe," teased Bianca.

I let out a long-held sigh and relaxed back into the joking rhythms of our usual conversations. We packed up the supplies from our ritual before heading to The Tilted Hollow to meet up with Hattie. I wondered what state she would be in, if she'd be her normal, bubbly self or the muted, dazed Hattie I saw the other night. Luckily, we got there before her so she wouldn't see us all arriving together.

We were huddled by the bar, ordering beers as

Hattie walked in the door, her face back to its usual cherubic, non-compulsioned state. Thank god.

"Hey!" she cried out, giving each of us a hug. "It feels like we haven't hung in ages."

"I know, you've been so busy!" said Bianca, trying hard to be casual.

"I know," Hattie said, apologetic. "Cas has just been making *so* many plans for us, it's hard for me to keep up with everything."

"How's everything going with him? Seems like you all are spending a lot of time together . . ." said Sage.

Hattie beamed. "It's going so well. I really like him. He's so good to me— treats me like a queen."

"Wow," said Bianca, trying to force a smile. She glanced at me, unsure of what else to say. We were all trying so hard to play it cool.

"And I know, *I know*, it's only been a few weeks, but it just feels right." Hattie was clearly so excited; it made my stomach turn. To think he was playing her like a pawn . . .

"What happened the other night, though? Sage and I thought you were going to join us for drinks after work but you rushed out of the store," I said, doing everything in my power to keep my voice calm and even.

"What? What are you talking about?" Hattie looked confused. "When was this?"

"Like a few nights ago? The end of last week. Sage and I popped into the plant shop and you were going to join us for happy hour, but then you suddenly had to leave."

"Oh, sorry about that . . . I got dinner with Cas that night I think." Hattie's face went from flustered to flushed. I couldn't tell if she was rattled at all by my question.

"Let's get you a beer," chimed in Sage, trying hard to smooth over any potential awkwardness. Sage glanced at me as if to tell me to let it go. I took a sip of my beer, letting its foam tickle my upper lip, trying to act cool.

Soon enough, we settled into our usual routine of talking a mile a minute, then hitting the dance floor until parched and ready for another drink. Nobody made another mention of Casimir or his coven. It was almost as if they had never come to town, like things were back to normal.

I was two beers in, leaning against the bar talking to Reina about glamours when the door flew open. A great gust of wind ripped through the bar. Jackson was there suddenly, and immediately found me. His face lit up. "How'd it go?" He leaned in and kissed me hello before giving Reina a hug.

"It went well, actually."

"Vi did great," said Reina as Jackson smiled down at me.

"I mean, we *all* did it."

"Yeah, but you were the one who transformed."

"I'm just glad it worked and you're safe," said Jackson as he put his arm around my shoulder and gave it a squeeze. "I was worried about you."

"You were?"

"Of course. I was pacing all over the loft earlier, trying to tap into anything that could be a warning. I was ready to run straight to the store if anything felt off."

"I don't know whether to be turned on or freaked out by that," I teased.

"I can't help it. It's wolf stuff."

"You're going to have to keep it together next week," said Reina. "We need everything to go as smoothly as possible." Her eyes stayed trained on Hattie, who was talking animatedly with Sage and Bianca. It was almost as if Hattie was completely back to her usual self.

"I'll do my best," Jackson said.

"We can't afford to have anything messed up. I don't know what would happen to her."

"She's going to be okay," I said, grabbing Reina's hand. "I promise."

"You can't promise that." Her brows were knitted in concern. This whole time we'd been too afraid to admit how worried we really were for Hattie. But we had to do everything we could to make sure she was okay and safe, free from the Trio's clutches.

I held her hand tight. "Maybe not, but I believe in us. We won't let anything happen to her."

"You're right." She sighed and her face relaxed some, but faint traces of worry remained.

CHAPTER FOURTEEN

The night of the undercover operation had arrived. My heart thundered in my chest as I stood in the tiled hallway outside of the Trio's meeting room. I swallowed hard as Jackson gave me a reassuring nod and opened the door. Adeline sat at a small folding table, looking up at me with a smile as I crossed the threshold. There wasn't an ounce of recognition in her eyes. I breathed slow and deep, willing my heart rate lower.

"Hello," said Adeline warmly. "Name?"

"Hi. Mindy Summers."

"First time?"

"Yes!" I smiled enthusiastically, channeling my inner Mindy.

"Were you referred to us by a friend?"

"Yes," I said, hesitant. "A woman from my yoga studio," I added, trying hard to stick to my story. Adeline nodded curtly and handed me a form. I sat down in one of the folding chairs, pen in hand.

A number of women were spread out around the room. A couple were also filling out newcomer forms, while a few small groups of women chatted. Each woman looked perfectly coiffed and manicured. They shared the same glossy hair that looked freshly blown out. Their bags were all perfectly conditioned leather in an array of designers. I spotted Hermès, Balenciaga, Fendi, and Marc Jacobs in one row alone. It was too hard to gauge an age range, as their skin was all taut and glowing. Not a wrinkle or pore in sight. And with my fresh new face glamoured, I blended in seamlessly.

"Hiiiiii," trilled a high-pitched voice. I put down my pen and swiveled around to see a petite woman in a slicked back bun lowering herself into the chair next to mine.

"First time?" she asked as she set her large leather tote bag on the empty chair on her other side.

"Yes," I said. "What about you?"

"Oh, I've been seeing them since they got to town a few months ago. My sister-in-law in Montreal recommended them. She looks 30. *She's 56*," she added in a hushed voice.

"Wow, that's incredible," I said, trying hard to feign enthusiasm.

"They're *miracle workers*," the woman said emphatically. "I'm Leslie, by the way."

"Mindy," I said, extending my hand to shake. A trio of gold bracelets dangled from her slender wrist.

"Great to meet you, Mindy. You're gonna *love*

them. Way more effective than any derm you'll find in the tristate area."

"Fabulous, that's what I need."

"Don't we all?" Leslie chuckled.

"Is everyone ready to begin?" called out a familiar alto voice. *Nikki.* Sure enough, she strode from the back of the room to the front and approached a makeshift altar.

A black lace tablecloth had been thrown across a folding table. Atop lay a pentagram with five serpent shaped candles, pale blush towers of rose quartz, rich green swirling chunks of malachite, tumbled turquoise stones, and palm-sized jade pyramids. I heard the door at the back of the room open and turned to see Casimir leading Hattie inside. She was under compulsion again, her eyes glazed over. Casimir steered Hattie to the altar, where Nikki and Adeline both now stood. My stomach tightened seeing her up there, next to those manipulative and conniving witches. I wanted to scream; instead, I clenched my fists as tightly as I could.

Adeline looked under the table and pulled out a small cauldron, lighting a candle underneath. She poured a bottle of water inside and stepped aside, motioning for Hattie to take over. Hattie glided up to the cauldron and opened her palm to Casimir, who reached under the table and pulled out bundles of dried herbs, flowers, and small glass vials. He set each ingredient neatly down next to the cauldron and Hattie began dropping them in methodically, stirring in different directions and muttering under her breath.

"The ceremony will begin now," announced Nikki. Behind me, Adeline turned off the lights. The room was dark, only the neon lights of Chinatown filtered in from the windows.

The women shifted in their seats, visibly excited. Some were already pulling out their wallets. Next to me, Leslie dug into her red Miu Miu wallet and pulled out a stack of crisp 100-dollar-bills. Adeline lit the candles with a long-stemmed match as Casimir began to chant quietly in something that sounded to me like Russian or Polish.

I glanced around the room at the women's rapt faces, now bathed in the flickering candlelight. Each one looked hungrily at the altar as Nikki began running her fingertips through the flames. Hattie continued brewing her potion next to Nikki, not a care in the world on her face. Adeline walked clock-wise around the altar, whispering to herself as she touched each crystal. The cauldron was now emitting a luscious golden steam. Nikki smiled upon seeing this and cleared her throat.

"Who would like to go first?" she asked commandingly.

"Me!" said Leslie, already half out of her seat. She had beaten a few other women whose hands were up in the air. Nikki nodded at her and Leslie strode to the altar.

Nikki placed one open palm against Leslie's

glowing face, her other hand cradling the back of her head. As Nikki did this, Casimir pulled out a large glass apothecary jar of dead bees and removed the lid. I knew immediately they were from Light and Shadow, just like Sage had said. He pulled out a handful of the glistening insects, tossing them into the cauldron's steam. As each tiny body hit the golden mist, they became reanimated. The sound of their buzzing wings filled the room as they hovered above the cauldron in front of Hattie.

Leslie stood perfectly still as Nikki removed her open palm. As her lips moved almost imperceptibly the bees began to swarm Leslie's face. I gasped and then slapped a hand across my mouth. Leslie began to shake, but Nikki's hand steadied her, cradling the back of her head until the bees all fell to the floor, dead again. The room was quiet except for the gurgling of the cauldron. Leslie's face was red and swollen. It looked so painful and I couldn't help but wince.

Adeline handed her a small glass jar of salve and Leslie returned to the seat next to mine, smiling. She began putting the thick translucent balm on her inflamed face. She exhaled as she rubbed the ointment in meticulously, and with each second, her skin became clearer, tauter, calmer. Her lips were now plump, her forehead smooth, her eyebrows lifted and perfectly arched. Leslie caught me gawking and smiled before leaning in and whispering, "Worth every fucking penny."

I swallowed hard, unprepared to go through with

whatever it was that I had just witnessed. Luckily, there were a slew of women eagerly awaiting a trip to the altar. Each one approached their turn with pride and reverence. I guess when you're already young, you take for granted the currency of youth these women were willing to pay for in pain and copious amounts of cold hard cash.

When I clocked three women left— four including me— I leaned into Leslie and excused myself. "Where's the restroom? I have to go before my turn."

"Second floor. Be quick!"

I grabbed my bag and hightailed it out of the room. Jackson was standing in the hallway, listening in. "Are you okay?" he asked, looking nervous.

"I don't think I can go through with this. It's crazy — they're reanimating bees to swarm women's faces. It's terrifying. We should get out of here."

"Violet," Jackson said calmly, grabbing my hands. "Deep breaths, remember?" I nodded as we inhaled and exhaled in time with each other. "I know you're afraid. But you have your amulet; you won't feel a thing. And I'm right outside. I won't let anything happen to you." He wrapped his arms around me and I let myself bury my face into his warm chest. His heartbeat was steady and reassuring.

"Okay," I said before peeling myself apart from him. "I'm going to get this over with— for Hattie."

"You got this, Vi. Don't ever forget how strong you are." Jackson said. I nodded, though I wasn't sure I fully believed him. "I love you."

"I love you too," I said, giving his hand a tight

squeeze. I walked back into that room alone, full of resolve. Sitting down, I made sure I was the next woman to raise my hand and, finally, approach the altar.

Nikki smiled at me as she began to cradle my skull with her hands. Her fingers were warm and tickling across my face like a spider's legs. I ran my own fingers over the cool stone of the amulet one last time as I steadied my breath, bracing myself for the bees. Nikki lifted her hand off my face and the bees surrounded me. Their buzzing was deafening as they stung my face chaotically. I could feel the pressure of them against my skin, but felt no pain. A surge of relief flooded my veins. Thank god for this amulet.

As each bee had fallen to the floor lifelessly, Nikki handed me my own pot of salve. I took it back to my seat and could see through swollen eyelids that Leslie was smiling excitedly at me.

"Get it, girl," Leslie whispered. I tried to smile but my face was so numb. I unscrewed the lid of the jar and dipped two fingers inside and began to smear the balm across my face. It was cool and awakened my face. My sight returned to normal as the swelling finally left my eyelids. Feeling returned to my skin as the salve sank in.

Leslie admired my face as the Trio's work was revealed. "You look *incredible*," she said in a hushed voice. I smiled and tried to nod politely as the last woman approached the altar. Once she was finished, the Trio and Hattie clasped hands around the altar, bowing their heads in silence. I scanned the room and saw that the other women had all done the same. I followed suit and lowered my head. But instead of closing my eyes, I did my best to keep my gaze on the altar.

After a moment of silence, the four witches dropped their hands and snuffed out the candles. Adeline walked to the back of the room, flipping the light back on. Sensing the overhead light, the women began to lift their heads and open their eyes. Each face I saw was smooth and dewy, youthful and jubilant, just as they had promised. The only indicator of their actual ages now were their clothing and mannerisms, and of course, their hands. The hands never lie; they betray age with a vengeance.

Next to me, Leslie was beaming, humming an upbeat tune as she counted her bills. "Can you remind me how much it is today?" I asked her.

"$1500," she replied without looking up. I did everything in my power to not balk and leafed through my tote bag. I found the envelope with the money in it that Sage had given me. Luckily, she had taken out $2000 as a precaution, not anticipating it costing anything more than $1000. Thank god, the store was doing well, and Sage was able to front the cost. We wouldn't have been able to go undercover otherwise.

Leslie got up from her chair, striding over to Adeline, cash in hand. Adeline smiled as Leslie handed over the stiff stack of bills. They said something to each other and shared a familiar laugh before Leslie came back to her seat.

Leslie picked up her leather bag as she leaned down towards me, her eyes intense. "You know, the Trio hosts other, more private events. They're a bit *exclusive*, but I think you should come to the next one," she said with an arched brow.

"Oh, really?" I asked, trying to smile. "What sort of events?"

Leslie's eyes began to twinkle as she lowered her voice. "Let's just say if you think your results tonight were amazing — and *they are*, honey — you will be in utter disbelief at what they can do for you when you join them for one of their salons. That's what they call them, salons. It's a little too tongue in cheek for my taste, but I really can't complain."

"Wow. Sounds incredible," I said, trying hard to not give myself away. "How do I get an invite? Once my husband sees me tonight, I know he'd be willing to foot the bill," I joked, hoping this sounded like something a rich woman living uptown would say. I couldn't screw this opportunity up. This was just the kind of opening we needed to figure out what exactly the Trio was doing behind closed doors with Hattie and how best we could free her.

"Please, my husband was practically begging me to keep it up after my first ritual," laughed Leslie. *Barf.* "Let me get your number. I'll text you if I get the okay from Adeline." She handed me her phone and I punched in my contact details. "Fab," she said, as she moved to head out the door.

"Well, it was great to meet you," I said.

"Likewise," Leslie smiled as she got up. "I'll see you soon, Mindy." And just like that, she strolled out the door, her face perfectly youthful and glowing.

CHAPTER FIFTEEN

J ackson was waiting outside for me. The other side of the street was teeming with tourists and hungry people in search of lo mein and Peking duck, Jackson buried in the crowd. I collapsed into his chest as he pulled me into a gap between two buildings.

"It's okay. You did great, and you're safe," he said as he handed me the antidote for my glamour. I took five drops on my tongue as Jackson held me, shielding me from any potential onlookers while the glamour faded.

"Thanks for being there for me. I don't know what I'd do without you."

"Vi, I would never let anything bad happen to you. Ever."

"I know." He leaned down and kissed my forehead as I wrapped my arms around his waist, letting myself melt into him. It felt so good to be held by him, to let him take care of me. I could finally relax.

"We should get going. Gotta meet the girls to debrief," I said, begrudgingly pulling away from him.

We held hands all the way home, through the streets of Chinatown and down onto the subway platform. I rested my head on his shoulder as we rode the train home in silence. I never wanted to let go of him after tonight.

When we reached Light and Shadow, the girls were already sitting around the table in the back room. A hot pot of peppermint tea sat steeping between them.

"How'd it go?" asked Bianca as she rose to hug me. "You okay?" Her big brown eyes were naked, no cat-eye liner, as she stared into mine. She looked so different. For a moment, I saw Bianca when we were eight years old and she was making sure I was okay after a bully had pushed me down at recess and she helped me back up. After calling him names and chasing him away, naturally.

"Yeah, I'm fine." I smiled and gave her hand a squeeze as I sat down.

"So how did it go?!" Sage asked as she poured Jackson and me a cup of tea.

"It went well— as well as it could have gone, I guess."

"Violet was amazing. She played it perfectly," said Jackson, smiling at me, proud.

"Tell us everything," said Reina.

And so, I did. I gave them the play-by-play of the evening and answered every minute follow-up question they had for me. Sage took down notes in a black leatherbound notebook as I tried to be as detailed as possible.

When I reached Leslie's invitation to the exclusive soiree hosted by the Trio, Jackson was the first to speak. "I don't know if you should do it," he said. He sounded resolute. "We have no idea what could actually be happening at these parties. This could be really dangerous. Leslie didn't give you any real information."

"Jack, we have to. For Hattie," I said. "We have to figure out what exactly is going on there and how to break the compulsion they keep putting on her." I knew he was just being protective, but my mind had already been made up. I was going.

"She's right," said Bianca.

"Well. I want the pack there with me so we can cover all angles of the brownstone." His jaw was clenched, his expression solemn.

"I think that's a great idea. We want to make sure you're as safe as possible, Vi." said Reina. The four of us girls nodded.

"Good," said Jackson. "I'm still not crazy about this idea, but at least with the pack there, we'll be in better shape."

Ding ding. My phone rang out from my bag with a text message. "I bet it's Leslie," I said as I pulled out the phone.

"What does it say?" asked Sage.

"'Hey Mindy girl, lovely to meet you tonight. I got the go ahead from the Trio. The next soiree is this

Sunday night since it's a new moon. Hope you can make it on short notice. Entry fee is 5k. Promise it's worth it — winky face emoji.'" *Barf.* Again.

"So that gives us only a couple days . . ." said Bianca, her brow furrowed. "Can we even do that?"

"Definitely," said Sage.

"Really?" I swiveled my head around to look at Sage. Her face was resolute, determined.

"Absolutely. I believe in us. We're such a strong coven. Our bonds are so deep. We won't let those witches tear us apart."

"Yes!" agreed Reina. "Hattie can't be caught in the Trio's web any longer."

"We need to get Hattie out of this mess ASAP," I said.

"Agreed," said Bianca. We all looked at Jackson expectantly. "This is for Hattie."

"Oh, I thought you were all having a coven moment. I didn't know if there would be, like, some secret handshake or chant or something. Didn't want to ruin it . . . but *yes*, obviously, I'm here for you all." I smiled at him and grabbed his hand across the table. Even with all this fear and excitement, he was still so cute.

"It's settled then," said Bianca. "Sunday is Operation Free Hattie." We nodded, feeling the gravitas and anticipation fill the room.

"I need a freakin' drink," I said.

Bianca started to laugh. "Don't we all."

"Let's go to the Hollow," said Jackson. "First round is on me." He slung an arm around me, pulling me next to him, tight. I relaxed into his side, letting the warmth of his body calm my frayed nerves and soothe the adrenaline that had been coursing through my veins.

I STEPPED out of the bar for a bit of fresh air after dancing hard with Reina. Bianca and Sage had parked it in a booth towards the back. I sighed into the night and wondered what Hattie was doing now. Was she back at the Trio's brownstone? Was she okay? Did she have any idea what was going on and that she was being used and manipulated? Just the thought of it made my stomach churn. My hands burned hot and angry.

The bar door swung open, letting out a quick burst of noise from inside. Sage strode towards me, holding up a joint. "Want some?"

"Sure." I could use the extra relaxation. Sage cupped her hands around the slim hand rolled cone, shielding it from the wind as she lit it ablaze with the flick of a fingertip.

She took a long drag and exhaled slowly. "Jack can't stop talking about how incredible you were tonight," she said before passing the joint to me.

"Honestly, I don't think I could have gone through with it if it hadn't been for him. I almost left, but he calmed me down when I considered making a run for it. Thank god he was standing outside that door . . ." I inhaled, letting the sharp smoke fill my lungs before releasing it into the night air.

"I'm sure you would have been just fine." I flicked a piece of ash to the ground as Sage studied my face. "You know that I think you're incredible too, right?"

"Sage . . ."

"I'm sorry, Violet, I just . . ." She held a hand to her face as she paused in thought.

"What?"

"I still think about that kiss, and I know I shouldn't but I can't help it." She exhaled loudly and reached for the joint in my hand, brushing my fingers. I knew it was on purpose.

"That kiss was a *mistake*."

Sage took a drag and nodded slowly. "It didn't feel like a mistake, Violet. I know you felt it too . . . that electricity between us." Her green eyes narrowed as she took a step closer to me. She reached out a hand to touch my arm, but I quickly brushed it aside.

"I'm with Jackson, Sage."

"I know."

"I love him, and I don't want to do anything to mess that up." Sage looked wounded as she flicked the joint and watched the ash fall to the ground.

"Okay," she said softly.

"I'm sorry. I don't want to hurt you either, but I just can't let myself get pulled into whatever . . . *this* is." Sage wouldn't meet my gaze, so I turned to head back towards the bar.

"Hey," she called after me. I paused, swiveling

back to look at her. "I don't want this to make the coven awkward."

"It won't, I promise. We're fine— we're good." I smiled at her as she nodded solemnly. I wasn't sure I believed that, but I needed it to be true. Whatever it was that had pulled me to Sage, that attraction and sexual tension, her allure, had finally all faded for me. The more time I'd spent with Jackson—the more our relationship had proven to be secure and right for me—the less I felt drawn to Sage. Maybe I'd used my attraction to Sage as a distraction from my fear of commitment to Jackson, my fear that I wasn't good enough to be loved—that I'd just screw it up. My heart sunk at the thought, but I knew there was truth to it.

Sage exhaled into the night air, her face dejected in the dim light. She tried to turn away from me, to hide her hurt feelings. I felt a pang of guilt, but knew we could never be together. It wasn't right for me, or her, or the coven.

"I really am sorry, Sage." I said softly.

"Me too," she said, her eyes downcast, face angled away from me. I hated that my own happiness with Jackson meant sadness for Sage. I watched the outline of her lithe body as she smoked, not looking at me, before I joined the others inside.

THAT NIGHT, Jackson crawled into bed, shirtless and sleepy. Letting out a long yawn, he held his arms out to me. "I'm exhausted," I said, mirroring his yawn as

I melted into his arms. I just wanted to be held close after such a high-octane day.

"Me too." He stroked my arm and I closed my eyes, content to be alone with him, finally. I debated telling him about what Sage had said outside the Tilted Hollow earlier, but it didn't seem worth it. All desire for her had truly faded as I finally trusted myself and my relationship with Jack. I wasn't ever going to jeopardize our future together again.

"You sure you're okay with going to that party undercover Sunday?" Jackson rolled over onto his side and faced me, his grey eyes wide and tender.

I threaded my hand through his hair, letting my nails scratch at his scalp. "Yeah . . . I just want this all to be over with. I want our old Hattie back and safe with us."

He pressed his soft lips into my forehead and kissed me sweetly as he rubbed my earlobe with his thumb and forefinger. "I know." He skated his long fingers up to my face and cupped my jaw. "We're going to get her out of there."

"We have to."

"We will, Vi. We will," he said softly as he leaned in and kissed me deeply. "You're a good friend. It's one of the things I love most about you."

"She's more than a friend. Hattie's my sister. The coven is my family." I didn't have siblings, but those girls were my sisters. I can't imagine blood ever being thicker than the bonds we shared. I'd do anything for them.

"I know, but that doesn't change anything. She'll

be ok. We'll make sure of it." Another long yawn escaped his lips, his eyelids hung heavy. "I love you," he said, quiet and almost asleep.

"I love you too," I whispered before nuzzling into his side. Burying my face into his shoulder, I took in his familiar scent that had begun to feel more and more like home over the past couple months. Everything about Jack made me feel safe. He fell asleep so easily, I suspected that was the wolf in him. His slumbering breaths punctuated the air like a low rumbly metronome. It was better than any white noise machine, as it lulled me to sleep ever so gently.

CHAPTER SIXTEEN

"Welcome, welcome!" said Adeline as the door to the Trio's brownstone opened. The smell of expensive candles and cleaning products wafted out as she led me inside. In the center of a foyer sat a table with a tray of champagne flutes. "Help yourself," she said with a flick of the wrist, her gold bangles jangling.

"Oh, thank you, but I'm okay right now," I said. Better to keep my wits about me. And who knows if that was pure champagne or if they had been laced with some kind of tincture.

"Suit yourself," Adeline said. I followed her into the parlor room that overlooked the darkened garden. A number of women milled about the space, many familiar from the ceremony before.

Leslie immediately caught my eye. She wore a floor-length billowing jumpsuit, its fabric emerald and silky. Her hair was slicked back in a chic and severe ponytail. She looked incredible—especially her glowing skin.

"Mindy!" Leslie cried out excitedly as she broke away from the women she had been talking with. "I'm *so* glad you came." She leaned in and gave each cheek an exaggerated air kiss as she clutched her half empty champagne flute.

"Thank you for inviting me," I said, flashing my most winning smile. "This place is fabulous."

"I know, right? And in *Brooklyn* of all places? I can't remember the last time I crossed the East River before these three came to town."

"Mmm," I murmured in agreement. Typical Upper East Side set, treating Brooklyn like another state.

"Come meet a few of the girls." Leslie steered me over to her two friends, both slender with vicious cheekbones. I wondered if the Trio had already worked their magic on these two. "Mindy, meet Kay and Melissa. This is Mindy, girls. It's her first time." Leslie gave me a wink and took a sip of her champagne.

"Nice to meet you," I said as they all smiled performatively.

"You're in for a treat," said Kay as her friend Melissa nodded enthusiastically. "You should have seen me before I met the Trio . . ." The three of them giggled conspiratorially.

"Oh, I'm sure you were just as beautiful before," I said, trying to be polite.

"I was cute, sure," said Kay. "But *now* I'm a work

of art." She smiled wide, showing off a perfect straight row of dazzling teeth so white they looked blue. Melissa and Leslie murmured in agreement.

"Show her your 'before' pics," encouraged Leslie with a nudge of the elbow. Kay dug into her mini Hermès bag and pulled out her phone. She swiped until she found the right picture, flipping over the display dramatically. My mouth dropped open.

"Oh my god."

"Told ya," she said with a smirk as I ogled the picture, my mind struggling to make sense of how much Kay had transformed thanks to the Trio's magic. She was right, she had been cute, but she didn't look like the woman who stood before me. There were aspects of her that remained the same— the distinct brown eyes, the slight upturned corners of her mouth, and the sleek raven shoulder-length hair— but gone were the round face, button nose, and thin, straight brows. She now had a defined jawline, slimmer nose, and thick, arched brows.

"It's incredible, isn't it?" cooed Leslie. I nodded in stunned silence.

"Ahem," came a man's voice from behind me. "Good evening, ladies." I spun around to see Casimir, dressed in a navy suit and holding a glass bowl containing a few cell phones. "Phones, please," he said with a smile. His accent seemed suddenly less pronounced, and I wondered if it was something he played up to charm Hattie.

We all carefully placed our phones in the bowl and Casimir whisked them away. I scanned the room, hoping to get a glimpse of Hattie, but she hadn't seemed to make her appearance yet.

Adeline moved about the room, chatting and charming her guests like a seasoned socialite. "She's so beautiful," remarked Leslie wistfully.

"Mmm," agreed Melissa as she sipped her champagne.

The whole energy shifted in the room as Nikki entered, draped in a floral crushed velvet spaghetti strap slip dress. It looked like some kind of vintage designer piece from the 90s, far cooler than anything I saw any of these other women wearing. Every eye seemed to follow her as Nikki began to circle the room.

But if I had stayed trained on her, I would have completely missed Hattie's entrance. She sat down in a corner armchair by herself. I felt lightheaded, anxious at the sight of her. She wore a flirty navy silk playsuit with a plunging neckline and black suede stilettos. I'd never seen her in any outfit like that—the Trio must have dressed her. She stared off into the distance with a slight smile fixed to her face. If any of these women had even bothered to notice her or talk to her, they may have thought she was drugged or on Xanax. I knew she was already under compulsion, and I fought the urge to approach her and drag her out of that brownstone right then and there.

Casimir appeared next to her, sans glass bowl. Hattie looked up at him and smiled adoringly. Cas traced the neckline of her playsuit, lustfully eyeing the deep crease of her cleavage. My stomach churned, disgusted and angry. I hated him with every fiber of my being. My fists clenched at my side as a sudden gust of violent wind rattled the windows overlooking the garden. A number of women gasped, sloshing their champagne in surprise.

Shit. I unclenched my fists and took a deep, controlled breath. I didn't need this night to go south before it had even begun.

Casimir looked at the windows, his heavy brow knitted. "Must be a storm rolling in. No need to worry," he said aloud to the room. With that, the women went back to their conversations unbothered. I let out a tiny sigh of relief as Leslie, Melissa, and Kay all chatted about some private school PTA drama.

Nikki was now talking to a tall redheaded woman who was already pulling out her wallet. The woman leafed through and pulled out a thick wad of cash, counting it under her breath before handing it over to Nikki. Nikki politely smiled and squeezed the woman's shoulder like a friend before approaching the next woman.

"Excuse me, I think I will actually grab a glass of champagne after all," I said politely to the ladies. They nodded in acknowledgment but continued their conversation.

I strode through the long foyer, heading for the front door. "Everything okay?" a voice rang out. I turned to see Adeline. Clearly, she had followed me out here.

"Just wanted to get a little fresh air," I said.

"Care for some company?"

"Oh, that's okay . . ."

"I'm in need of a smoke," she said. "Don't tell anyone." She winked as she swung the door open for me.

I scanned the street for signs of Jack or the pack and caught a glimpse of Malin's ice blonde hair in the distance, a number of houses down. The tightness in my chest released, just a little bit.

"Don't be nervous," Adeline said as she lit the end of her cigarette delicately. *Shit*. She could sense my discomfort. *Chill out, Vi.*

I sat down on the top step of the stoop as Adeline leaned against the iron rail, smoking. She looked so glamorous, like a Parisian supermodel. "Everybody's nervous the first time. But really, there's no need. It's over in a short minute."

"What's over?"

"You'll see," Adeline said with a jovial wink. She exhaled slowly, letting the smoke unfurl from her mouth like a ribbon. "You're going to love the results. That's what matters, right?"

I nodded and tried to smile politely as I dug into the pocket of my trousers. My fingertips found the cool stone face of the amulet. I grasped it tight, letting it crease the flesh of my palm. "I think I'll head back in," I said, standing up. "I still need to pay."

"Don't tell *any* of those women I smoke. I know it's not a good look, but damn, it feels great." Adeline took a long drag as she watched me carefully.

"Of course. It'll be our little secret." She gave me a half smile and I turned on my heel, eager for this night to be over. I wondered when the ritual would finally begin.

Nikki approached me the minute I entered the parlor. "Hello," she said with a smile, her voice as velvety as her dress. "Mindy, right?"

"Yes, hello." I extended a hand. Nikki's fingers were adorned in an assortment of dainty gold rings.

"Nikki. I'm so glad you could make it."

"Me too. Leslie spoke so highly about it, albeit she was a little cryptic. I'm not entirely sure what to expect."

Nikki let out a soft chuckle. "Ah, but that's part of the fun, isn't it?" She arched a perfectly groomed brow.

"I guess so." I'm sure these women with their perfect manicures and planned out lives did get a real thrill from the occult. I can't imagine realizing for the first time, as a grown woman, that there was magic lurking underneath the placid, polished surface of their lives.

"Don't be worried," Nikki said, squeezing my arm. Her hand was ice cold. "I do need the payment, though."

"Oh, of course." I opened my bag and rifled through its cluttered contents until I found the envelope with the $5,000 portioned into crisp hundred-dollar bills. I handed it over. Nikki opened it, silently counting the bills.

"I don't mean to be gauche," she said, catching

my gaze. "Looks like we are all set . . . please, help yourself to some champagne. Enjoy your evening." She flashed me a beguiling smile and glided over to the next victim.

Leslie waved me back over to their little group. "I think it's going to start soon," she said in a hushed but excited tone.

Casimir circled the room, collecting the champagne glasses. Melissa quickly downed the rest of her drink and handed it off. Leslie and Kay's were already empty and they practically tossed them aside. The three of them exchanged giddy little smiles. "Are you excited?" Melissa asked me.

"Of course," I said, forcing myself to look happy. "How could I not be?"

I glanced to the corner and made sure Hattie was still there. She was seated quietly by herself, her face unmoving. Kay caught me eyeing her and leaned in. "She's new. I don't know her name, but it seems they may no longer be just a trio."

"More like a quartet," added Melissa. Rage bubbled inside me, but I swallowed hard trying to quell it. Hattie would *never* be a part of their coven. They would never be a quartet; I'd make damn sure of it. I thought of Jackson and took a deep breath, imagining he was there with me. I didn't need another windows-rattling moment. Couldn't risk the Trio sensing something was up. Since I seemed to be the only new soiree attendee tonight, they would immediately know I had something to do with it.

"Whoever she is, since she started working with

them, my skin has been way brighter and firmer. My crows' feet are staying gone for way longer," said Leslie. Kay and Melissa murmured in agreement. "And it's *way* less painful."

The lights suddenly dimmed as the Trio, with Hattie by Casimir's side, gathered at the front of the room. The chatter quieted as everyone turned their attention to them. "Let's begin," said Adeline. The four of them turned and began to walk into the hallway, their guests snaking behind them.

Leslie grabbed my hand and gave it a squeeze as she flashed me a wink. We followed them down the hallway and through a doorway to the lower level. Each woman carefully descended the stairs, careful not to trip or twist an ankle as they teetered in their high heels.

The basement was cavernous and dim, only lit by candlelight. A series of half-height windows faced the quiet street, but thick black drapes blocked any semblance of the outside world. A dark wooden round table sat in the middle of the room with candles dripping artfully as they flickered. And then I saw it— that crystal dagger that Bianca and I had seen weeks ago upstairs. I felt my heart jump into my throat. It was displayed in the middle of the table. The candlelight illuminated its jagged edges and reflected light off it chaotically.

The women formed a wide circle mirroring the table, and I took my place between Leslie and Melissa. The air felt thin, as if we were at a high altitude. I plunged my hand into my pocket and fingered the amulet again. I thought of Jackson, waiting for me outside. Protecting me. *Everything would be okay. Everything would be okay. Everything would be okay.*

I exhaled slowly as we all clasped hands. Nikki spoke first, her eyes closed as if in prayer. "In the absence of the mother moon, we comb the shadows and purge all that is ugly and unwanted. For when the light shines upon us again, all that remains is beauty." Her eyes opened and the candle flames doubled in size. The room was now bathed in an amber light.

Adeline broke away from the circle and approached the table, lifting up the crystal dagger. "Who would like to go first?" The tall redhead stepped forward confidently. She had no hesitation. Adeline nodded as the woman extended her arm towards her, palm facing up. She took the woman's hand and held onto her long, slender index finger. Adeline smiled at her as she took the dagger, placing its sharp crystalline point into the pad of her finger. Blood pooled at its tip as the woman stood stoically, watching Adeline mutter incoherently under breath.

Then Casimir appeared at Adeline's side with an ivory chalice, the phases of the moon carved into its smooth surface. Adeline guided the redhead's finger to the chalice and tipped it over, letting the blood fall into its basin. I reluctantly pulled my eyes away from this scene to find Hattie still in the circle next to Nikki, face serene and eyes glassy.

CHAPTER SEVENTEEN

The chalice made its way halfway around the circle, steered by Casimir and Adeline as they pricked each woman's outstretched finger. I did not like blood magic, not because of its gore, but because it felt backwards and slightly barbaric. It wasn't something to be trusted. I was always taught blood sacrifices were archaic and inhumane. But these women all seemed to be consenting, and more than one seemed almost thrilled to be partaking in something so visceral.

I didn't want to give them my blood, but as the chalice came closer and closer to me, I realized there was no way out. When they reached Leslie, she thrust her hand out, eager, her palm flaring and fingers spread wide. The sharp jagged tip of the dagger pierced the soft flesh of her hand. My heart began to thunder in my chest and I felt as if I could hear each candle flickering cacophonously in my eardrums. My right hand clutched the talisman in my pocket. Its edges dug into my palm as I forced my left hand out towards Adeline, who smiled reassuringly. Every neuron in my brain was firing at full speed, willing my legs to run and carry me away as far as I could get from here.

Adeline raised the crystal dagger above my finger as I braced for the cut. My jaw was clenched and the muscles in my chest so tight they ached. Adeline pressed the sharp point into the pad of my finger. I almost gasped expecting pain but was taken aback when I felt nothing. The amulet burned in my right hand instead, still buried in my pocket. I could feel it taking the pain from me. Just as I hadn't felt the swarm of bees, I didn't feel the slice of the blade. I watched as the blood rose to the surface of my finger, red and sticky and shining. Adeline let it pool and then twisted my hand so the blood fell like a heavy rain droplet into the chalice to join the other women's offerings.

They moved onto Melissa next to me as I examined my finger. The puncture wound was angry and began to coagulate. When every woman had been pricked and given their blood sacrifice, Casimir placed the chalice back onto the table. Nikki stepped up to join her coven, and Hattie followed robotically. Anger flared inside me again, burning hot in my stomach. Casimir trained his eyes on Hattie as she took a large amber vial from the table. She uncorked it, her lips moving silently as she said an incantation to herself before pouring the vial's contents into the chalice.

Nikki took the crystal dagger from Adeline and raised it above her head. In the candlelight, her face looked sunken, her features exaggerated by the shadows cast by the flickering candles. She inhaled sharply and began speaking, her voice less like velvet now and more like stone. "Blood for blood, spilt and taken for rebirth. We give you this gift as you have given us yours, so that we may be born anew." She manically dragged the blade across her palm, carving a line across her flesh. I gasped, but only Leslie seemed to notice. She side-eyed me and I took that as my cue to not to show any more signs of freaking out.

Blood began to trickle down Nikki's hand and onto her forearm, like the hot wax dripping down the candles. She reached her open palm out over the chalice and let the blood flow into the cup before handing the dagger to Adeline.

Adeline now raised the dagger up high and repeated, "Blood for blood, spilt and taken for rebirth. We give you this gift as you have given us yours, so that we may be born anew." She sliced open her hand just as Nikki had and let it bleed into the chalice. Casimir took the dagger and followed suit, reciting the spell and offering his own blood. My heart beat in my ears, the thumping making my head feel like it may explode. Casimir handed the dagger to Hattie who lifted her arm up as if being pulled by an invisible marionette string.

I fought the urge to scream out "No" and tell Hattie to stop. The room began to swirl and I didn't know if I was going to faint or vomit. I clutched the amulet in my pocket as hard as I could, feeling its cold silver dig into my skin. My breathing was shallow and ragged as I tried desperately to calm myself. *Inhale, exhale, inhale, exhale.*

Hattie drew the blade's edge across her open palm, tracing it gracefully like a skate on ice. Her eyes were blank and empty. The Trio was taking her blood against her will. Without her consent. And they knew the power it held. They'd sought her out for the very gifts she bore, present in her red blood. Sweet Hattie who only ever wanted to find love and help and heal people with her herbal magic. My skin was prickly hot as I tried to bite down my rage. I wanted to make them pay.

Nikki picked up a small tin of salve on the table and rubbed the ointment into her palm, before passing it along to Adeline. Their wounds healed before our eyes from the soothing balm Hattie had no doubt expertly concocted. Leslie shifted her weight next to me. I looked over and saw her glowing in the amber candlelight, a greedy smirk stuck to her face. Casimir took the chalice and walked it over to the tall redheaded lady who'd begun the ritual. She delicately placed her fingers on the stem and helped him guide the goblet to her lips.

With a single sip, she began to writhe uncontrollably. "Aaaeeeeeeeeeeeee." She let out a bloodcurdling shriek. Her body contorted painfully as everyone watched silently. My pulse was racing at breakneck speed. I'd lost control of my breathing completely. I knew a panic attack was setting in. I scanned the other women's faces, desperate for help or recognition or someone to put an end to this woman's pain, but everyone stood by stoically. Only a few seemed to wince or grimace, but nobody appeared shocked or worried. *What the fuck was happening?* My breath caught in my chest, ragged and tight, as the windows began to rattle.

The room began to tremble, as the redhead went quiet and still. She fell to her knees, catching her breath. She looked up and smiled, her face youthful and new. It was too late, though, the windows shook harder and faster, feeding off my quick panicked breaths. A few women in the circle shifted in their heels nervously. Casimir urged the women to continue and held the chalice up to the next woman's lips. She took a sip and began to convulse, howling with pain.

My heart was thundering in my chest when the windows suddenly shattered, tiny shards of glass burst apart, spraying everywhere. Women began to scream and covered their beautiful faces protectively. The dark drapes billowed into the room as a gust of wind ripped through the air. The basement erupted into chaos as another gale tore through the windows, so strong it knocked over the burning candles, setting the velvet tablecloth ablaze. Everyone screamed at a fever pitch, running towards the stair-well. I felt frozen and all I could think of was to find Hattie. I could see her standing still among the mayhem, her compulsion unbroken. The flames engulfed the table in a roar, obscuring her now completely from me.

As women knocked each other over to get up the stairs first, I tried to skirt around the burning altar to get to Hattie. I was suddenly yanked back by a strong familiar arm. "*Violet,*" screamed Jackson's voice. I spun around and saw his panicked face. "*We have to get out of here.*"

"I'm not leaving without Hattie!" I shouted over the raging fire. It was going to engulf the entire room any minute now. In a split second he nodded and dashed across the room, dodging the violent flames as they licked the air. He threw her over his shoulder and ran to the closest front window, hoisting her up.

"Violet, get out, *now!*" I scrambled to the closest window and pulled myself through, scraping my arms bloody from the broken glass. A stiletto fell from my foot into the basement as I crawled away.

"Fucking high heels," I yelled, taking the other shoe and throwing it into the blaze before darting over to Hattie by the other window. *Wait- where was Jackson?*

"Violet, I can't get through!" Hattie was blocking the majority of the half-height window.

I pushed her unmoving body as she stared off into the distance, slumped against the facade of the brownstone. "*Hattie, move.*" I begged. I used all my strength to shove her out of the way. Jackson's long muscular arms appeared on the ground suddenly as he crawled through the window—just as the drapes caught flame. His face was dirty and the hem of his jeans looked singed. I threw my arms around him and held him tightly as sirens wailed.

"Jack! Violet!" Fiona called as she ran over to us. Malin right behind her. I looked to the stoop and saw Desi, Gabe, and Athena had kicked in the front door and were helping the women down the stone steps. These perfectly coiffed women, now wild and terrified as they flooded onto the sidewalk. The street began to flash red as a firetruck barreled around the corner and screeched to a halt in front of the brownstone.

"Where'd the Trio go?" I asked Jack.

"I don't know, I wasn't paying attention to them. I just needed to get you and Hattie out of there." I turned and ran to the stoop in my dirty bare feet.

I rushed up the steps, as the final disheveled woman left the brownstone. Gabe tried to say something but I waved him off as I ran inside. The floor was hot from the fire below but the flames hadn't seemed to spread upwards yet. I ran through each room of the house and then upstairs, opening every door I could find. I searched every closet and tore back every shower curtain in a rage. The Trio was nowhere to be found.

CHAPTER EIGHTEEN

Hattie sat on the curb, drinking a cold bottle of water as Fiona stroked her back. A cluster of the women stood in stunned silence as firefighters rushed into the brownstone.

"You really don't remember *anything*?" I asked. Hattie looked up at me, her blue eyes wide and lost, and shook her head slowly. I could tell she had been crying.

"That must be so scary," said Fiona quietly, her hands still on Hattie's back.

"It's just all blank . . . the last thing I remember was sitting down in their kitchen and having a cup of tea. Casimir made us a pot of earl grey . . ." Hattie set down the water bottle and buried her head in her hands. "I'm such an idiot. I can't believe I thought he really loved me."

"Oh Hattie," I said, crouching down beside her and wrapping my arms around her. She leaned into me and I felt her crying. "You're not an idiot. You didn't do anything wrong. He's a terrible person who conned and manipulated you."

The pack were gathered around us, their faces lit by the flashing red lights of the firetrucks. I held onto Hattie as we sat on the sidewalk, across from the Trio's brownstone. Together, we watched the firefighters wielding their hose, spraying the ground floor. The flames slowly died down, until it was just thick ribbons of smoke unfurling from the shattered windows.

Jackson pulled the glamour antidote out of his pocket and I suddenly remembered I was still Mindy. In all the commotion, I'd totally forgotten. I dropped the elixir onto my tongue. The glamour melted as my features morphed back into my old familiar face. The pack watched in stunned silence. Desi and Gabe's mouths were agape.

"That is sick," muttered Athena.

"Does that hurt?" asked Malin.

"No, it just feels like pressure kind of." They all looked at me like I was a rare animal in a zoo, with awe and curiosity.

Jackson let out a soft chuckle, before changing the subject. "Where do you think they went?" he asked.

"No idea . . ."

"You said they'd moved here from Montreal?" asked Desi. I nodded.

"But they wouldn't go back there," said Hattie as she swiped at her tear-stained cheeks. "I'm guessing they will have gone somewhere very far away where nobody knows them. Somewhere new."

"Yeah, I have a feeling this isn't the first time they've done this," I said.

Sirens began to wail louder and louder until three cop cars turned onto the street, lighting up the night in blue and red. Neighbors along the street were watching the commotion from the safety of their own stoops by now.

"We should get out of here," I said, standing up and pulling Hattie to her feet. Beside us, the pack nodded, murmuring in agreement as we walked towards the subway and took the train back to Bushwick to Light and Shadow.

The girls were all waiting for us, nervous, at the shop. Sage opened the door and Bianca immediately rushed to me as Reina grabbed Hattie.

"You all look like hell," said Bianca.

"What happened? Are you okay?" asked Sage.

Reina guided Hattie to a chair in the backroom as we all settled in, the pack and coven coming together like attendees of an important summit.

"Are you okay?" Reina asked Hattie, her face riddled with concern as she brushed Hattie's dirty blonde hair out of her eyes. "Do you remember anything?"

"No, nothing . . . I only just came to on the sidewalk after the fire."

"Fire?!" Reina cried, snapping her head to me.

"Yeah . . . so we have a lot to talk about." I

launched into a thorough retelling of the evening's events, from my first steps into the parlor to the crystal dagger and blood sacrifice to the panic-induced window shattering and ultimate firestorm. Sage took meticulous notes as everyone peppered me with questions about the day. By the end of the evening, I was exhausted and depleted. All I wanted to do was crawl into bed with Jackson and fall asleep in his arms.

"Do we think they'll ever turn up here again?" asked Bianca as the clock turned to midnight.

"No, I doubt it," I said with a yawn. "But . . . who knows." I felt eyelids get heavy. Hattie sat quietly next to Reina, who was stroking her hair like a mother soothing her daughter.

"I think we should call it a night," said Sage, setting down her pen. Everybody began to say their sleepy goodbyes. I leaned into Jackson's chest. "Take me home," I whispered. He squeezed me hard and then called us a car. Bianca, Jackson, and I rode back to the apartment in silence after making sure Hattie was okay one last time. I knew Reina would take good care of her, of course, but I didn't know how Hattie would process the deceit and betrayal of being under compulsion.

Bianca hugged me tenderly before heading into her bedroom. "I'm glad you're okay," she said softly. "I love you."

"I love you, too."

Jackson led me into my bedroom and turned

down the covers. I peeled my clothes off and let them fall to the floor before crawling into bed. My body was pulling me under, begging me for rest. Beside me, Jackson stripped down to his boxers and slipped into bed beside me. Pressing his soft lips into my forehead and then my lips, he sent me off to sleep.

THE NEXT MORNING as we sipped our coffee in bed, Jackson's phone dinged with an update from the New York Times. He inhaled sharply as he scanned the alert.

"What?" I asked.

"'Brooklyn Heights Cult Ritual Gone Wrong, Leaders On The Run.'" he read aloud.

"Oh my god," I gasped. "What else does it say?" I leaned into him as he brought up the article for us to read.

"'Wealthy yoga moms in search of the occult ends in chaos and flames after being swindled out of thousands of dollars,'" Jackson said, reading aloud the tagline.

"Oof," I sighed. We read the article pressed into each other. His body was warm and reassuring, even as I relived the night before. It felt like a bad dream, but the scrapes on my arms from the shattered glass said otherwise. Last night had been very real.

"I hope Hattie's doing okay today." Jack reached his arm around me and held me close.

"I hope so too" I thought about Hattie sitting in her apartment with Reina, and was grateful she had one of our sisters to care for her this morning. I wished I could make it all better for her, erase all the hurt and betrayal she was feeling. She deserved so much better.

"Thank you for everything yesterday," I said, kissing his shoulder.

"Violet, you don't need to thank me."

"You saved us. Hattie and I could have died last night in those flames."

"I would have never let that happen," he said, his face serious. "And you would have never let that happen to Hattie."

I shrugged my shoulders, still unsure. "I totally panicked."

"Anyone would have, Vi. That was a terrifying situation. I can't imagine what was going through your head."

"Thank god you were there, Jackson."

"You know that I will always be there. I will *never* let anything like that happen to you again. I don't know what I'd do without you."

"I don't know what I'd do without *you*," I said, staring into his grey eyes.

I cradled his face in my hands, his days old scruff tickling my fingertips, and kissed him slowly. Our lips lingered on each other sweetly. He hooked his arm around me and pulled me into him tightly before flipping me over on my back. We kissed deeply, intertwined on the bed in the dappled morning sun.

SIX WEEKS LATER, I sat in McCarren Park watching Hattie toss a pale pink frisbee with Reina, Bianca, and Sage. I leaned my head on Jackson's shoulder and smiled as I saw Hattie start to laugh, mouth open towards the sun. She'd struggled in the month that followed the Trio's disappearance, and still sometimes had night terrors about them. But she was doing so much better and had even started dating again. Her usual ebullient light had begun to shine again.

"You wanna join them?" Jackson asked. "I've gotta head to Threes for my shift."

"Aw," I said with a teasing pout. "Yeah, let me go show them how to really work a frisbee." Jackson rose to his feet and pulled me up with a little hop.

I tilted my face up to him and we kissed goodbye. "Go easy on them, my sylph."

"I'll do my best." Jackson flashed me a cheeky smirk before walking towards Williamsburg. I took a moment to admire his broad shoulders as he strode down the footpath, before running to join the girls.

"Think fast!" cried Bianca, lobbing the frisbee at my head. I swiped it away like a prickly cat.

"So athletic," teased Sage.

I stuck my tongue out and picked the disc up. "I'll show you athletic!" I chucked the frisbee as hard as I could and it spun through the air far over their heads.

Hattie laughed and began to run after it. "I'll get it!" Her smile was wide and carefree.

"Get it, girl!" Reina called after her.

We all watched her and I could feel a collective sigh from the coven. Our beautiful, positive, happy Hattie was back and smiling, and our coven was stronger and closer than ever.

ACKNOWLEDGMENTS

A big thank you to Emily Berge for your keen eye, encouragement, and generosity. I'm so very grateful.

And another big thank you to Kara— my romance queen— for all of your advice and helpful feedback. This book is so much better because of you.

Thank you to my biggest cheerleaders: Hayley, Morgan, Jamie, Chantel, Joanna, Rebecca, and Paige. Your support and excitement for this book has lifted me up and kept me going, even when I doubted myself. Thank you for all the texts, calls, drinks, and laughs.

Many thanks to Roman Belopolsky for your amazing cover design and all the beers you've bought me over the years.

Thanks to all my friends (*you know who you are*) for your love and support. I'm so blessed to have you all in my life. I love you so very much.

And no acknowledgements would be complete

without gratitude to my parents, Bob and Cathy. I would not be who I am— or the writer that I am— if it weren't for you two. Thank you for your unconditional love and unwavering faith in me. I love you more than words can say.

ABOUT THE AUTHOR

Kit lives in Greenpoint, Brooklyn with her scruffy rescue dog. When not writing, she's dancing around her kitchen unironically to Lana Del Rey, pining for Van Leeuwen pistachio ice cream, or soaking in the bathtub until devastatingly shriveled. *A Crystal Dagger* is the follow-up to her debut novel, *A Violet Wind*.

Sign up for her mailing list at kitearnshaw.com to stay up to date with new releases.

 instagram.com/kit.earnshaw

Made in the USA
Coppell, TX
04 November 2021